BREAKING 80 AT 80

A STORY ABOUT A ROUND OF GOLF

WES ST. CLAIR

Paperback: ISBN 978-1-7348970-6-7

Ebook: ISBN 978-1-7348970-7-4

St. John Publishing Company
P.O. Box 1291
Pleasant Grove, UT 84062

Cover art by Andra Judd

Photo of Wes St. Clair by Scott Hancock

Background portrait: William St. Clair, Captain of the Honorable Company of Edinburgh Golfers (1771) by Sr. George Chalmers

PRAISE FOR BREAKING 80 AT 80

Every golfer will identify with the main character's mental challenges in trying to break through to a new level of performance. St. Clair also shares interesting perspectives on the single-plane swing within the unfolding drama of his hero's mission.

DR. JOE PARENT, BEST-SELLING AUTHOR OF
ZEN GOLF: MASTERING THE MENTAL GAME

Good golfers quickly realize that their accomplishments have as much to do with their mental game as they do with the physical tools they are using. That "inner fight" is on full display in Wes's book. A fun read for all golfers.

PAT J. POHLEN, PGA CLASS A, HEAD PRO
RIVERVIEW GOLF CLUB AND GRAVES GOLF
MASTER INSTRUCTOR OF THE MOE NORMAN
SINGLE-PLANE SWING

Another "lessons learned" and entertaining story by Wes. Worthwhile for any golfer who wants to consider another option.

FRANK MCGINITY, AMATEUR GOLFER AND
AUTHOR OF *GET OFF YOUR STREET*

A great story and a good read... entertaining and instructive.

A most enjoyable story with some good tips and challenges along the way. I was anxious to see if the main character reached his goal.

Breaking 80 at 80 is a wonderful, fun read and offers a different take than most golf books. It puts the reader into the mind of what many of us golfers have been through - the trials and tribulations of our sport.

This is a great story of a man's journey to accomplish a goal he has set for himself. It was fun to read about Jack's experience hole-by-hole and to meet the people that he encountered along the way. A really nice tale which shows that if you give yourself an objective, you have a chance to make it happen.

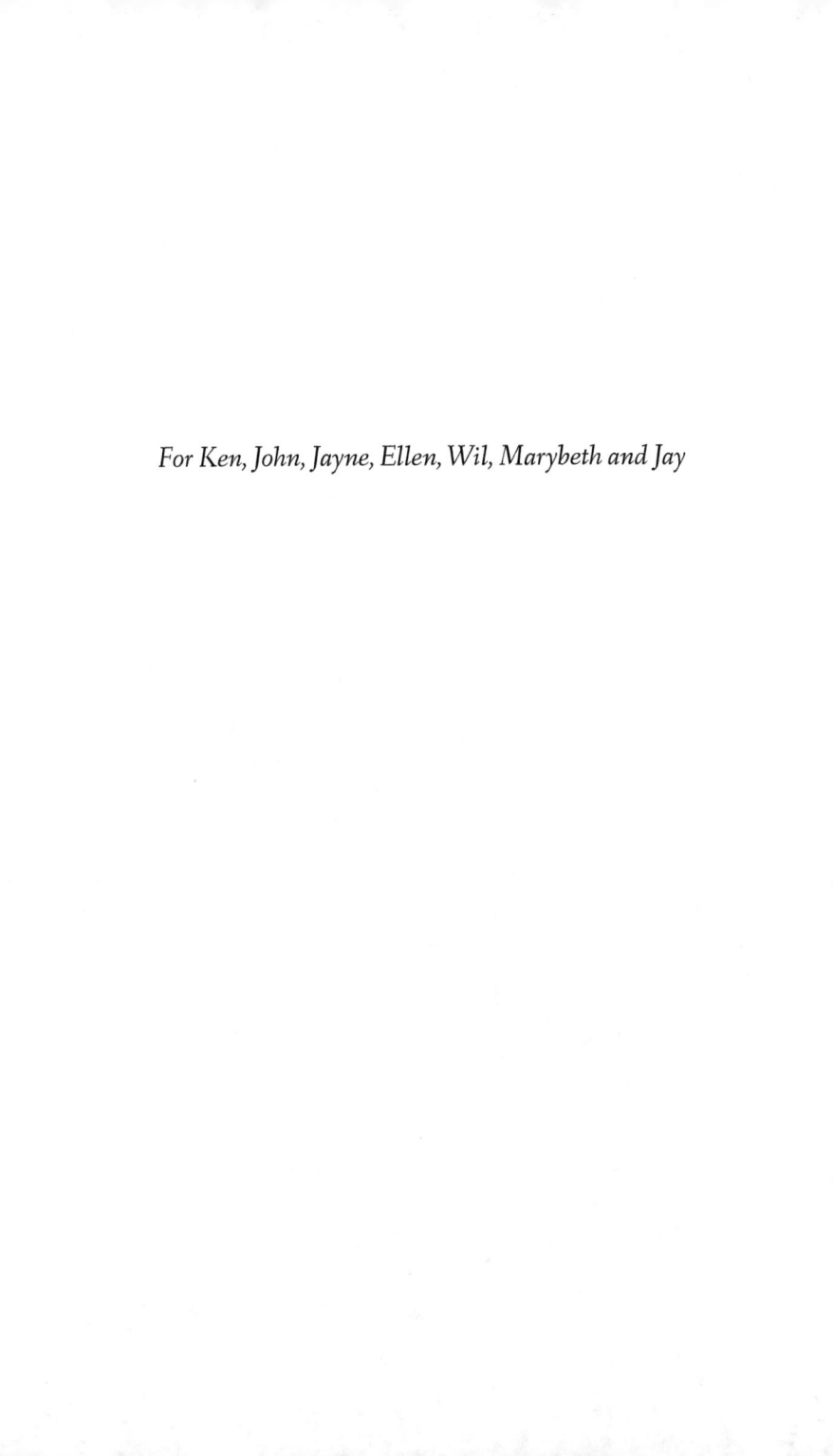

For Ken, John, Jayne, Ellen, Wil, Marybeth and Jay

CONTENTS

Author's Note   ix

THE FRONT NINE

Chapter 1   3
Chapter 2   10
Chapter 3   15
Chapter 4   21
Chapter 5   24
Chapter 6   28
Chapter 7   32
Chapter 8   36
Chapter 9   41

Interlude: The Halfway House   47

THE BACK NINE

Chapter 10   53
Chapter 11   57
Chapter 12   60
Chapter 13   64
Chapter 14   68
Chapter 15   72
Chapter 16   76
Chapter 17   81
Chapter 18   86

Chapter 19: The Club Room   93
Chapter 20: The Hogan Room   99

References and Recommended Reading 107
Who Was Moe Norman? 109
Acknowledgments 111
About the Author 113

AUTHOR'S NOTE

My inspiration for this book came from watching golfers for many years - golfers who pursued the sport despite their continued frustration with the game. What inspired them to keep playing? Was it the fresh air or the companionship of their playing partners? Their desire to experience the perfect swing or one par? These are powerful motivators, but for most golfers, they become overshadowed over time by a growing dissatisfaction with one's tools or one's own competency. I witnessed friends continuing to play out of sheer habit rather than pleasure, and it caused me to wonder: was this current of negativity hardwired into the game itself, or could a change in perspective or technique help rekindle a love for the sport again?

This book serves to highlight the techniques that worked for the main character, Jack, in his attempt to break free from the cycle of frustration and disappointment that plagues so many us golfers. It is not meant to be a manual of instruction. There are many competent instructors and books that can teach you more about the single-plane swing, and hopefully this tale will inspire you to seek them out.

Good luck on your journey to a more enjoyable game of golf.

Wes St. Clair

February 2022

THE FRONT NINE

ONE

"Success depends almost entirely on how effectively you learn to manage the game's two ultimate adversaries: the course and yourself."
Jack Nicklaus, American Professional Golfer

Eighty years.

8 – o. Those numbers had preoccupied Jack Santee all the way from his home on the seventh fairway, looming larger in his thoughts than the oaks that lined the country club's entrance road. Unconsciously, Jack eased his foot off the golf cart's accelerator and drifted slowly beneath the overarching sentinels.

These trees had weathered more than eighty years of California storms, infestations and drought. They possessed far more dignity and grandeur than he did with his eighty-year-old physique, yet they held their limbs high and stood at attention, saluting the former Air Force officer as he went forth on his mission to conquer the course of eighteen holes.

To fit the occasion, Jack had worn his favorite green golf shirt with the club logo along with a matching hat and a pair of freshly-pressed tan slacks. He felt he was dressed like a winner, and all omens pointed encouragingly in his favor as he pulled into the parking lot. The early morning weather was a comfortable seventy-two degrees, with clear skies and not a hint of wind. The sparseness of vehicles meant the golf course wouldn't become congested anytime soon.

As he stepped out of his golf cart, the sign on the main building caught his eye: "Old Oak Country Club". That suited him. He was an old oak himself. He probably had more in common with the trees along the entrance road than the low-handicap players that hustled from hole to hole on Sunday afternoons. He'd just take his time and see what the game wished to give him on his 80th birthday.

"Hello, Mr. Santee," said the club attendant. "Headed for the range?"

"Yes, Larry. But I plan to play 18."

"Great idea, Mr. Santee."

Jack wanted to say more, but he bit his tongue. No sense jinxing it. The less pressure he put on himself, the better he'd play. But the importance of today's game kept intruding on his thoughts as he approached the practice tee. Eighty years old... no better day to break eighty. And it sure would make for great cocktail talk at the clubhouse.

Jack's friends had wanted to join him on the links to celebrate his birthday, but he preferred to golf solo on this occasion. Few knew of his quest to score under eighty. He was always trying, but never came close. That sense of frustration had led him to a local teaching center called High-Tech Golf where he'd worked steadily with a pro named Ralph Williams over the last twelve months. Jack had polished his technique enough to improve substantially at the center and practice range, but his actual play was limited. Ralph had pestered him to play more, and he probably should have done so in the buildup to today's game. Nothing he could do about it now.

Jack took out his wedge at the practice tee, drew a calming breath and swung. The ball flew perfectly, as if he were guiding the arc of the tiny, white sphere with his mind. That was reassuring. A few more hits, and then he moved on to the 8-iron, followed by a 7-wood, a 3-wood and finally, a driver. Each time, he could scarcely believe his accuracy. Jack couldn't recall if he had played on his birthday before, but turning eighty seemed to be one hell of a good-luck charm.

He gave some of the credit to another instructor, Carl Johnson, who had taught him the single-plane swing a few years back. The man didn't possess the high-tech gadgetry they had at the teaching center, but he'd been able to successfully show Jack how to bring the club back down on the same plane he took going back. The swing had been pioneered and perfected by the Canadian golfer Moe Norman – one of the best ball strikers of all time – and Jack was sold on the technique, as it gave him better ball contact than with a conventional swing.

The next stop was the practice putting green. Here, Jack's sessions with a golf psychologist really came into play. Dr. Michael Feinstein had worked with Jack to take his ego out of the game, helping him achieve a degree of calmness while on the green. Jack's friends teased him for constantly starting sentences with "Dr. Mike says", but on this morning, at least, the effects of the doctor's consultations were undeniable. Everything he hit on the putting green was going in. His jitters and self-doubt were steadily fading into the background.

Five years ago, Jack had been a different golfer - erratic and unconfident. But now he possessed new skills with his single-plane swing, new techniques from his mentor Ralph and a new mindset from Dr. Mike. If he was going to pull off a sub-80, there would be no better day than today. Time to approach the first tee.

As Jack selected his driver, he tried to maintain the state of mind he felt at the practice putting green. Of course, Ralph's mantra, "Just play golf," cycled once or twice through his thoughts. The first hole was a par 4, but played like a par 5 since it was the number one handicap hole. His personal handicap was 17, though he was unsure about the accuracy of that number since he hadn't posted a score in over a year. He'd played a few holes during that time, in between lessons and practice sessions, but never a full round.

Jack placed the ball and assumed his position on the tee. The air was still calm, which was to be expected in Southern California at this time of day. He went through the motions a few times, pulled back, and swung. The ball sailed out over the fairway, and time seemed to slow for just a few seconds until the ball landed and rolled to a stop. Over 200 yards. This might be his day to break 80 after all.

He drove his cart down the fairway to his ball and checked the distance: right at 235 yards. One of his best. 185 yards remained, although a creek lay between Jack and his destination. He could take the risk and try for the green, or he could simply make his usual 100-yard shot down in front of the creek. Though his confidence level was high, he decided to play it safe. Hopefully, his third shot would get him onto the green, so he'd be putting for a par or a bogey – still a good score for this hole.

Jack took out his wedge and swung. Unfortunately, the ball pulled to the left and almost rolled into the creek. So much for confidence.

His next shot would be 80 yards to the green, but the angle was poor. He was left of the green and the pin was on the left side. He spent almost a minute thinking over his options until Ralph's words popped back in his head: "Just play golf." *Right.*

For the distance required, Jack knew he had the perfect club – a gap wedge that had always served him well on the practice tee. He swung away and made great contact this time. The ball flew high in the air, traveling a good distance but still landing 25 feet from the pin. Not as close as he wanted, but still good enough for a chance at par.

He lined up his putt, sensing it would break to the right. Jack's instincts had served him well lately on the practice green, and the speed of his putts had usually been sound. He got himself in position, swung smoothly, and was relieved to make perfect contact with the ball. It had a good roll, but contrary to his assumption, the putt broke to the left and ended up to the side of the hole. At least his speed saved him; the ball was only a foot away from where he needed it to be.

He was left with an easy tap in. Still, he made sure to draw on his "Dr. Mike" mentality this time before sending the ball across those last few inches. A bogey. He could live with that, since this was supposedly the hardest hole on the course.

One down, 17 holes to go. Same number as his handicap. He caught himself starting to make scoring calculations in his head and forced his mind to stop; it was way too early for that.

Instead, he considered the question of whether he should analyze the rights and wrongs of his golfing strategy on each hole or wait until he finished the 18. Ralph would probably have something to say about it, but then again, perhaps the coach's three-word slogan was only applicable while Jack was actually playing.

He pulled a water bottle from his golf cart and decided he would review his game after all. With his goal of breaking 80, Jack needed every advantage he could get. His drive on the first tee had gone well, and all he could remember about the moment was that he had kept his mind a blank while hitting the ball. His second shot should have been a simple lay-up, but it had gone poorly. After watching video playbacks at the High-Tech Golf Center, Jack had learned that these types of failures usually came from his old habit of swaying. Ralph Williams had worked with him on this, reminding him to keep his weight on his left foot and to straighten his right knee during his backswing. That technique had worked well for Jack in the past, and it might have helped him this time if he had remembered to take a couple practice swings beforehand.

His third shot was 80 yards to the green, and he couldn't see any reason why he didn't land closer to the pin. So Jack forced himself to drive back in his cart and recreate his approach shot. After lining himself up, it became obvious that his alignment was 25 feet off. He simply hadn't taken the time to check it.

Returning to the green, Jack expected to find that his alignment on the first putt had been similarly flawed, but after close examination, he realized that he had failed to walk around the hole to determine exactly how the putt broke. At eighty years old, Jack thought he should have learned a thing or two about patience.

These were all issues he could fix, or at least he stood a chance of addressing them. Jack knew that a sub-80 score wasn't going to come easy; in all likelihood, it would be the hardest birthday present he ever tried to give himself. And a second, incontrovertible fact loomed at the back of Jack's mind: he wasn't getting any younger. Still, he felt grateful to be out in the fresh air on such a beautiful morning, whatever result awaited him at the end of eighteen holes.

He sat behind the wheel of his golf cart and pushed the accelerator. On to hole number two.

TWO

"Only two players have owned their swings: Moe Norman and Ben Hogan."
Tiger Woods, American Professional Golfer

As Jack drove off from the green, he spied a father and son positioning themselves at the first tee, and he wondered if he'd have to let them play through at some point. For a moment, his memory flashed back to his first dabblings with golf almost... *wait... had it really been seventy years ago?*

Back when he was at elementary school in Indiana, his dad introduced him to the sport, and Jack managed to talk his parents into spending money for a few lessons at the local country club just so he could maintain an edge against his seventh-grade buddies. His interest didn't last for too long, mainly because the Midwestern heat on summer afternoons could be oppressive, and he hadn't been an early riser back then. He fell back into golf midway through his teenage years, scoring well enough to land a place on the high school B team, but he admittedly lacked the discipline to practice and improve on his own time, outside of school.

Jack attended ROTC in college, earning himself a 2nd Lieutenant commission from the Air Force along with his marketing degree, and upon graduation, Jack was assigned to an airbase in North Carolina for two years. Good fortune followed him from Indiana, for he landed a plush management job at the officer's club right out of officer training. Civilians ran the club, so Jack didn't have much to do apart from signing checks and greeting officers and their wives. That left plenty of time for golf and parities.

His game had benefited from the mildly competitive atmosphere on the military base. Unfortunately, that all changed when he left the Air Force and took a marketing job in New York with one of the biggest advertising agencies. As a trainee, he didn't have much time for golf, plus it was too expensive to play at the better courses. The bright side of that busy time was that he managed to meet Marie Anderson – the woman who would become his wife one year later.

Jack rose through the ranks at the agency and was assigned to the Sports Division, which counted a golf club manufacturing company among their clients. Within a few years, he was placed at the head of the division and guided it through a period of rapid expansion. In time, Jack felt confident enough to strike out on his own, and several clients followed him, including the golf manufacturer. He founded his own firm with three employees and limited capital, but over the decades, Jack cultivated his client base and grew his business into one of New York City's largest agencies. Eventually, he was able to sell to his partners and retire with his wife to Old Oak, California. Buying a home on a golf course had been his idea, naturally. He smiled, thinking about *that* negotiation.

Returning his focus to the present, Jack parked beside the second tee and examined the terrain with fresh eyes. The next hole was 380 yards - a par 4 and a handicap of 9, with a slightly elevated green at the end of a long straightaway. He pulled out his driver and took a couple of practice swings to make sure the sway in his stance was gone. Then he checked his alignment since the tee box was not lined up with the fairway. It would be too easy to land out-of-bounds.

Everything seemed in order until he suddenly noticed two people guiding their pushcarts underneath an oak tree on the right side of the fairway. They got themselves situated, raised a golf umbrella to protect themselves from stray balls and waved for him to proceed. If Jack had been able to send word, he would have told the couple that they'd be safer standing in the middle of the fairway, since most golfers sliced on this hole toward their exact position.

After studying their outfits, Jack realized they were acquaintances of his – Bennie and Deb Pierson. The couple had continued playing golf into their nineties and were easily the oldest living members of the Old Oak County Club. If they had a chance to learn about the single-plane swing, Jack thought they would welcome it, since it was much easier on the lower back.

After verifying his alignment once again, Jack swung away, and the tiny orb flew high, straight and far. He climbed back into the cart and checked the distance when he reached his ball. Right at 195 yards. Jack pulled off his cap and scratched the back of his head. He could have sworn he'd made a solid hit that time. The ball should have traveled further. Well, he'd just have to figure out the reason for the short distance later. He called out a thank-you to the Piersons for letting him play through, then brought his attention back to his second shot.

185 yards remained, same as it had been with the first hole. The fairway wood seemed like the right club for the job, as it fell somewhere between a 3 and a 4-wood. He took two more practice strokes, making sure his right knee was straight on the backswing. Then he connected. Off went the ball, straight on line with the pin... but it landed 20 yards short.

What went wrong this time? Jack knew he had used the right club, and he had accounted for the elevated green. His mind started to go into analysis mode, but he forced himself to pull back. There'd be time for that later. If he was still going to get a par, he needed to focus on the work at hand.

The next shot looked straight and uphill, but he remembered this time to walk up and look around the hole. Sure enough, from the left side the green appeared to slope down from the mountains. He could account for that. His next decision was whether to make a chip or a pitch shot. Jack determined that a chip shot with an 8-iron would be better, as he'd have more control and there would be less of a chance of falling short. He'd rehearsed this movement plenty of times at the training center: weight on the left foot, stay still, check alignment and swing with a putting stroke. A few more practice swings, and he connected. The ball took off on the right line, curved towards the hole but stopped two feet short.

Everything's coming up short on this hole, he groused. But at least he was close. He could still get a par. The putt was uphill, and he already knew it broke to the left, but he checked around the green to make sure his initial assessment was correct. By his estimate, he needed to aim the width of one hole to the right of his target, and he also had to account for the uphill so that he wouldn't fall short again. He would make it in this time. But just to be sure, Jack drew some slow breaths, as Dr. Mike suggested, to allow any dissatisfied thoughts to leave his mind.

He took a smooth swing, and the ball turned into the hole but bounced out. Another bogey. Jack couldn't help but stay optimistic. His inner cheerleader glanced at the scoreboard in his head and began to chant, *"Only two over par,"* ignoring the fact that Jack had played just two holes. No matter. What he had learned earlier about doublechecking both his alignment and the contours of the green had benefited him on the second hole. Fixing his swaying habit had helped too.

He still couldn't figure out why he kept falling short with his distances. Jack wanted to put more thought into it, but decided it was best to press on. As long as he was striking the ball well, he could let the distance issue go for now. Maybe his breakfast would finally kick in and provide a boost of power somewhere along hole number three.

THREE

"The definition of insanity is doing the same thing over and over again and expecting different results."
Rita Mae Brown, American Author
(Often Misattributed to Albert Einstein)

Dr. Mike would have chastised him for dragging his ego into the game, but as Jack drove to the third tee, his mind kept focusing on what people would say when he walked into the clubhouse later this afternoon. His wife had reserved the Hogan Room for a birthday gathering, including cocktails and dinner. Jack expected that his close circle of friends would show up to wish him a happy 80th birthday - ten or a dozen people at most. Of course, his golfing buddies would probably dispense with the pleasantries and ask straightaway how his round went. He hoped he'd have a good story to tell them.

If Jack came up short in his quest to break 80, his wife wouldn't love him any less. Marie could always put things into proper perspective. When they first moved into their home on the seventh fairway, she'd made friends with other non-golfers at the country club while Jack quickly latched on to a new group of golfing companions. After several months of their new routine, Marie shared an observation: she had noticed how Jack would leave to play a round of golf with great enthusiasm, only to return several hours later in a pessimistic mood. She wasn't trying to be malicious or mean-spirited with her words; after five decades together, Marie simply wanted Jack to be happy. And she sincerely couldn't grasp why anyone would invest that much time in an activity that consistently failed to satisfy them.

Jack admitted that she had a point. He couldn't remember seeing that pattern among golfers in his younger days, but after Marie's comment, he began to notice the same downward emotional trajectory more and more often in his fellow players at Old Oak Country Club. There had to be a baseline level of insanity inherent in the sport if people didn't enjoy golfing but felt compelled to return to the course again and again for four hours at a time. The more Jack thought about it, the more he realized that he was missing something about golf. Unless he wanted to completely change his lifestyle, he had to figure out what that missing element was.

He felt he was halfway there. Hard work and a new attitude had made all the difference. His coach Ralph at the training center had pressured Jack to put in the hard work, and his golf psychologist had helped him adjust his outlook on the game. He hoped he could maintain that degree of zen detachment when he faced his friends at the end of eighteen holes.

The third hole was a par 3 with a handicap of 17. At a mere 125 yards, it had to be the second-easiest hole on the course. The green sloped back toward the fairway and was well bunkered, with a front center pin. Jack had played this hole two different ways when the pin was in this position. He could either hit long and plan for the ball to roll backwards toward the hole or he could aim for the fringe in front of the pin. His success had been better when he hit short, so he decided to play it safe.

He wavered, however, on whether to choose a 7 or 8-iron. Normally, his 7-iron would take him 130 yards and the 8-iron would go 120. He knew the distance of 125 yards to the pin was still accurate, even though the pin was up front, because the tee markers were back. He selected the 8-iron and took a few practice swings. *This could be a perfect shot, easy,* he thought.

He got set up to the hole, but at the last second, the word "distance" popped into Jack's head. It refused to leave, needling at his concentration. He started second-guessing all his preparations, so he forced himself to back off the tee, clear his mind and get set again with a little more composure.

This time, Jack achieved what he felt was a perfect swing – great contact, with the ball flying high and curving to the left as it descended towards the pin. It landed ten yards too long above the hole, which was *not* what he'd been expecting. Hitting 135 yards with an 8-iron was rather unusual. He'd been planning on taking his next shot from below the pin, but at least he wasn't falling consistently short like he had during the previous hole. Perhaps his breakfast had kicked in after all.

Now Jack faced a downhill putt of 30 feet. The contour was straight, but the necessary speed proved harder to judge. He got set up, then tried to allow for the downward slant as he took a gentle swing. The ball had a good roll, right on line, but its speed proved to be too much. It missed the hole by an inch and continued to travel another ten feet.

That left Jack with a ten-foot uphill putt if he wanted to save par. He already knew it would be a straight shot; all he had to do was swing like it was an eleven-foot putt to account for the gradient. He got set up and made good contact with the ball as usual. It headed straight for his target, but three inches from the hole, the ball made an inexplicable right turn and came to rest ten inches away.

Where in the world did that come from? Now Jack was trying to save a bogey when he had started out putting for a birdie. His confidence was flagging, but he shook it off the best he could and made the ten-inch putt. That gave Jack the distinction of making a bogey on the second-easiest hole at Old Oak Country Club, and it left him 3 over par. He was playing bogey golf and matching his 17 handicap. At this rate, he would be lucky to break 90. He had no choice but to analyze what went wrong and hope he could make up for the errors in due course.

At the tee for the third hole, Jack had hit well but overshot the pin by 10 yards. His 8-iron had given him 135 yards instead of the usual 120. He tried to reference his state of mind at the time; certainly, he'd been thinking about distance and about all the shots that had fallen short on the second hole. Had he simply overcompensated?

It occurred to Jack that whenever he experienced a string of short shots at the practice facility, Ralph Williams would instruct him to increase the speed of his swing to gain more distance. His coach kept pushing him to swing faster – not quicker or harder by making jerky movements, but by using even acceleration. The change in technique was frustratingly subtle, but Jack had practiced moving his club fast back and then fast down to the ball, and the results had been better contact and more distance.

Unfortunately, those skills were still fresh enough that he wasn't applying them consistently. His anemic performance on the second hole was proof of that. Jack promised himself that he'd be more conscious of his speed in the future... at least until those movements became second nature. Maybe he'd pull out his 9-iron to make 120-yard shots next time if he managed to keep his improved swinging consistent.

The other thought that crept into Jack's mind was that when he was on a real golf course instead of a practice range, he might have to adopt a different mindset. Aiming for a specific destination on a fairway wasn't quite the same as "hitting balls to nowhere" at High-Tech Golf. Here, every swing mattered for something. He was accountable for his victories and his mistakes. Perhaps a little extra concentration might be required, even if it came at the cost of some of that "zen" Dr. Mike had been pushing.

The next step was to examine his first putt. He walked up to where his ball had landed thirty feet from the pin, then sized up the scene. Immediately, Jack knew where he'd gone wrong. He hadn't picked out a spot halfway to the hole, aimed for that location and allowed the ball to roll the rest of the way. More than one of his coaches had stressed that tactic, he felt embarrassed to recall.

Finally, he looked at the ten-foot putt that had cost him his par. He had assumed it was a straight uphill shot because the downhill putt from the other side had been perfectly straight. But as he looked around the hole, Jack saw a small mount that had made the ball curve to the right. Once again, he had forgotten to do due diligence, and he felt so frustrated he wanted to whack himself in the head with his putter.

He couldn't continue having three-putt greens and bogeys if he was going to break 80 today. Some real soul searching needed to happen before he moved on to the fourth hole. He was forgetting too much of his training.

Maybe the real challenge of golfing at 80 years old was the memory issue, he considered. His excessively-powerful 135-yard shot at the top of the hole had proven that his muscles had woken up. Now he needed his brain to do the same.

FOUR

"Ninety percent of this game is mental and the other half is physical."
Yogi Berra, American Baseball Player and Manager

Jack resolved to keep his mind more focused for the remainder of the game. *Maybe I should stop thinking about breaking 80,* he considered. He had read somewhere that anyone who attempted to predict a score was bound to have a bad round. Perhaps a few tips from Dr. Mike would help to reorient his thinking. Two of his coach's mantras came to mind: "breathe" and "trust in your swing". He hadn't thought much about his breathing so far, and he admitted he still may have been guiding his club rather than letting go of his intentions.

Hole number four offered a chance to rectify these mistakes. It was 363 yards from the middle markers with a handicap of 7 and a par of 4. It featured a dogleg to the right and traps on the right-hand side as the fairway turned. He knew the best drive lay left of the traps with a good angle to the green. If he tried to cut the corner and didn't make good contact, he could end up in one of the traps or fall short with no clear shot to the hole.

Jack emptied his mind and took a couple of practice swings. Then he recalled his intention to breathe. He inhaled deeply several times and swung once more for good measure. He set himself up over the tee, checked his alignment and tried to remember the feel of the last practice swing. As expected, he made good contact; the ball flew straight and landed right where he'd wanted it to be. He caught up to the ball and checked the distance: 220 yards. That left 143 yards to the center of the green.

The remaining distance was perfect for his 7-iron - the club he had used in practice more than any other club. Jack felt confident about this shot, but he still did his usual routine and cleared his thoughts before swinging away. The ball had a good trajectory, sailing high and arcing left towards the hole. It landed ten feet to the right of the pin. Jack thought the ball would continue to roll in the direction of the hole, but it came to a stop.

At last, Jack thought, *I'm putting for a birdie. Don't screw it up by being short or long and struggling to save par... or a bogie.* His poor performance on the last hole leapt easily into his mind, and suddenly Jack realized he was setting himself up for failure. He was creating negative images in his head by invoking the word "don't" - a word Dr. Mike had warned him never to use. Jack got all the chatter out of his mind and replaced it with an image of his ball rolling into the hole.

By the time Jack reached the green, he was feeling pleased with himself at having upped his mental game. His training was coming more easily to mind before every swing, and he hoped to apply that discipline to the holes ahead, beginning with this one. He started by examining the green from all sides. The putt was level and it broke slightly to the left, which he could detect from the opposite side and the left side. To compensate, he decided he should aim for the right edge of the hole.

Jack followed his usual routine, keeping a light grip on his putter and maintaining a mental image of the ball reaching its destination as he swung. The ball had a good roll and kept right on line as it turned left and stopped on the right edge. Jack waited for it to fall in, but the ball refused to surrender to gravity. He gave it a few more seconds in case it could be persuaded to change its mind, then he sighed and tapped it in for a par.

Jack was okay with a par. He had come close to making a birdie, and he was only 3 over par overall. Of course, he still had fourteen holes to go...

As he headed for the fifth tee, Jack gave himself a quick critique. His first two shots had been excellent; he had stuck to his routine and trusted in his swing. His putt had been as accurate as one could be without the ball actually going in the hole. But one question occurred to him: had the image of the ball reaching the right edge of the hole been stronger in his thoughts than the image of the ball rolling into the hole? The ball had gotten hung up on the edge, after all.

Perhaps he was just playing mind games with himself, but it occurred to Jack that he could have more clearly pictured the right edge as a *path* into the hole, rather than as a destination. The distinction was something he could focus on in the future. At the least, it wouldn't hurt to try.

FIVE

"There are no absolutes in golf. Golf is such an individual game, and no two people swing alike."
Kathy Whitworth, American Professional Golfer

The fifth hole was another par 3 with a handicap of 5. Jack remembered how he'd fooled himself into thinking the last par 3 would be easy. To avoid making the same mistake, he needed to maintain an attitude that there were no easy holes.

This hole in particular had been his downfall on many outings. It was only 130 yards, but the green was guarded by a lake on its right front side and a creek to its immediate left. The natural tendency of most golfers was to aim left of the hole, but that sometimes created a pull towards the left sand trap and the adjacent creek. As it was with most shots, the whole idea was to hit the ball straight.

The tee was elevated and the pin lay at the back of the green. After taking those factors into account, Jack thought the situation called for an 8-iron. The 7-iron would be too long, and the 9-iron wouldn't be long enough. He took his usual practice swings, got himself set up, then let it go. To his amazement, the ball ended its roll three feet to the right of the pin. Jack was ecstatic; this would be his first birdie.

He knew he had his clubs to thank for moments of accuracy like this. They were a gift from the golf equipment company that had defected to his new marketing firm when he left his former employer and struck out on his own. His client insisted on giving him a new set every year, along with a dozen balls, because they considered him one of their best ambassadors, and the gifts hadn't stopped coming after he'd formally retired. Each set of clubs was top-of-the-line and fitted to his specifications, which meant that he couldn't blame his equipment whenever shots went awry.

As he climbed back into his golf cart, Jack noticed another cart several fairways over that was heading towards the seventeenth green. He had to squint because, for a moment, he thought one of the two men in the front seat was his old single-plane golf trainer Carl Johnson. But he was mistaken. Carl, he remembered, lived fifty miles south of Old Oak and was known for never straying more than five miles from his home and local golf course.

Seeing Carl's likeness brought to mind the refresher course Jack had taken from him last week in anticipation of today's round. Carl had noticed that Jack consistently made the same mistakes with his feet and club position at set-up. The trainer instructed Jack to maintain a more open position with his left foot and a more closed position with his right. Also, Jack was told to keep his club further back at set-up. In Carl's presence, Jack had hit a few shots with the club only 6 inches back, but he needed to be at 10-12 inches in order to keep his club low. Both suggestions had improved his game.

Those thoughts led Jack to reminisce about the single-plane golf school he had attended earlier this year. His coach for the three-day program was Danny Murphy - a former college baseball player and businessman who had retired early and become certified as a professional golf instructor. Danny had been a top amateur golfer for many years, and his lessons had emphasized the importance of the lower body in relation to the arms and hands.

Suddenly, Jack realized he had arrived at the green. He had lost track of time, thinking about lessons and other tangents after promising that he would keep his thoughts concise and focused on his next shot. Especially *this* shot, where a birdie was at stake. He was beginning to sound like a broken record. A quote popped into his head, though he could not remember its author: "Whatever you resist will persist." He needed to stop dwelling on his previous flaws and find a way to calm his wandering mind.

Jack stepped onto the green and looked over his putt. It appeared to be just as he expected - three feet away and level, but he double-checked around the hole anyway. He didn't want to be fooled again; this was a chance for his first birdie of the day, after all.

He took a couple of practice swings with his light grip, then set up and took the putter back. While keeping his thoughts clear, he made good contact with the ball and it went straight in with just a moment's hesitation at the end. *A perfect television putt,* Jack thought. Now he was only two over par for the day.

As Jack prepared to head out for the sixth hole, he assessed his latest performance. He hadn't put much thought into his putting so far, so he focused on that aspect. Putting skills were something he had developed on his own over the past year, and he had adopted a similar set-up as the single-plane swing, positioning his hands and arms straight out and shifting his weight onto his left foot. Over the decades, he had also learned the importance of holding still, which helped him keep the club-head square on the ball.

Jack's biggest area of improvement recently was in controlling the ball's speed. By accident, he'd discovered that if he extended his right arm as he finished, his putting distance greatly improved. So far today, his new skill set was serving him well. Hopefully, opportunities for additional birdies would be forthcoming and plentiful.

SIX

"*You swing on two planes. I swing on one. My move is simpler. I have fewer moving parts.*"
Moe Norman, Canadian Professional Golfer

Jack arrived at the sixth tee and surveyed the terrain. 470 yards, with a par 5 and a handicap of 13. The tee was elevated, which always felt like an advantage, whether that was true or not. He doubted he was gaining any real benefits from elevation here; this hole required a straight shot due to the out-of-bounds territory on both sides of the fairway as well as the sand trap that lay waiting about 200 yards on the left.

It occurred to him that he had avoided getting caught in any sand traps so far. *There I go again,* he immediately said to himself. *Setting myself up for failure by focusing on the negative. Got to toss that thought away.* He pulled out his driver and took a couple of practice swings to clear his mind. Then he took the shot. His contact was good, and the ball sailed straight across the fairway, landing just to the right of the sand trap – a distance of slightly over 200 yards. Not a bad position for the next shot.

As he drove down the fairway in pursuit of his ball, Jack spotted two golfers in the distance walking off the green. He felt mildly surprised since he assumed no one else had been ahead of him. If he had to guess, Jack thought they might be the Club President and the Club Champion. He didn't need to worry about asking if he could play through; they were fast players and would soon be out of sight. He wondered what they would have thought of the single-plane swing, and then he quickly answered his own question: *I've never known a golfer who wouldn't consider a swing change if he thought it would lower his handicap.*

Jack's next play was about 160 yards, and if he landed in the right area, the ball would roll an additional 10-15 yards and stop in front of a pond with a level lie. If he landed in the *wrong* area, not only would he be further back, but he'd end up with a downhill lie. He knew what he had to do here. His ability to achieve that goal, however, was uncertain.

Trust yourself, Jack thought as he took out his 7-wood. That club was good for 160 yards. He got all set but backed off quickly after an idea flew into his head. One of his many coaches had once told him, "Take the time to see the shot. Don't just visualize where it's going to land." Jack went back behind the ball and took that advice. He tried to see the shot. He tried to paint a complete picture in his mind, and though he wasn't an artist, he did his creative best. When he finally swung, the ball took off and landed exactly where he had envisioned, ten yards from the shore of the pond.

The 75-yard shot to the green felt perfectly designed for his gap wedge. The pin lay on the left side of the green, close to the bunker, and to reach it, Jack had to get his ball over the pond successfully and make sure that it stopped short of the sand trap.

He felt remarkably confident despite the challenges. His contact on all his previous shots this morning had been consistent, and he knew that the trajectory of his gap wedge shot would be high and stop on the green. Also, water hazards were no longer a mental obstacle; he had shed himself of that anxiety years ago.

He swung, and the ball took a flawless trajectory toward the pin. It came down just past the pin, but it didn't hold up. Instead, the ball continued further, right into the clutches of the trap.

Jack wished he could have erased his earlier thoughts about his luck with sand traps, but he didn't feel too concerned. As he drove up to the green, he was reminded of another golf school he had attended many years ago where he'd spent an entire day hitting balls out of different traps. *No time for those thoughts now,* Jack said to himself.

Although bunker shots had always been within Jack's scope of expertise, this particular shot still looked challenging. He would be attempting it while positioned only twelve feet away from the pin. Jack got himself ready, following the particulars of his setup routine: an open stance, with his weight on his left foot and an open club face. He used a single-plane swing and made good contact. The ball burst out of the trap with a splash of sand, just like on television, but then to his dismay, the ball landed and rolled twenty feet past the pin in the opposite direction.

Jack closed his eyes and took a deep, slow breath to settle his nerves. He now faced a twenty-foot putt to save par. Thankfully, the putt was level; it would be a simple matter of getting the speed right - something Jack had a fair amount of success in doing this past year.

He took his stroke. The putt had another good roll straight towards the hole, but he came up three inches short. A wave of disappointment washed over him as he tapped the ball in for a bogey. *It's a crime to be short on a putt,* thought Jack. *What happened?* Now he was back to being 3 over par.

On route to the seventh tee, Jack initiated his usual review. He'd hit the ball so well on the last hole, only to end up with a bogey on a hole with a handicap of 14. It should have been an easy par or a possible birdie. He knew the bunker shot had presented a high level of difficulty; he didn't fault himself too harshly for the poor result. But to be short on the putt was inexcusable.

One explanation came to him: since he'd been long on the two shots before the putt, maybe his subconscious had pushed him to not be long for a third time. *Who knows,* Jack said to himself. Perhaps he was overanalyzing everything. As he arrived at the seventh tee, Jack held firm to his positive outlook. 3 over par was not too bad for six holes, and he looked forward to tackling the final three holes of the front nine.

SEVEN

"There are certain things you can't control on the golf course, like the weather, course conditions, and your playing partners."
Unknown

The 7th hole was a par 4 with a handicap of 15 that arced uphill for 375 yards to an elevated green. Along the fairway, Jack saw three players approaching their second shots, but they were too far away to identify. He hadn't noticed them before now; maybe they had started on a different hole than the first one. Either way, he hoped they'd be moving fast enough so that he wouldn't have to play through them.

Focus on the task at hand, he reminded himself. To have any chance of reaching the green on his second shot, Jack knew he'd have to start things off with a good drive. Thankfully, his first shot went beyond the 200-yard marker and straight.

He waited for the trio of golfers to start clearing the fairway before heading in their direction, and as he drew closer, Jack couldn't believe what he was seeing. The three men were none other than his best friends and old golfing buddies, John McGuire, Bob Winthrop and Harry Baker. Even though they were all on great terms, these were the last people that Jack wanted to run into. He had declined to play with them this morning because of his goal of breaking 80, but there they were anyway – Harry and his pull cart leading John and Bob's cart towards the green. *My worst nightmare,* Jack thought. He took a deep breath and tried to put the situation into perspective. *Can't forget, it's only a game.*

Jack reached his ball and checked the distance. *225 yards.* He thought it would have gone further, but the uphill slant of the fairway would explain the shortfall. That left 150 yards to the pin in the center of the green, though the elevation would make the distance play longer... about ten additional yards, he estimated. Once again, one of his favorite clubs, the 7-wood, would be perfect.

Jack took a couple of practice swings, then glanced up at the green and saw his friends waving for him to hit. Apparently, the guys had recognized him as well. They were waiting for his next move before they made their putts. Jack wasn't happy about having an audience, especially people who knew him personally and were curious to see his new swing technique. *Well, you're stuck with the situation,* Jack told himself. *Just trust your instincts and hit the ball.*

He forced himself to take a moment to visualize where he wanted the ball to travel. The green broke to the left and he knew he had to aim for the right side past the hole to allow for the slope. Without further deliberation, he took the shot. The ball sailed through the air, landed six feet to the right of the pin and rolled to the left about a foot. His buddies let out a roar of approval followed by vigorous applause. Jack shook his head in disbelief. *Maybe having an audience isn't as bad as I thought.*

When Jack arrived at the green, his friends seemed delighted to see him. He politely asked if he could putt first and move on, but John suggested, "Why don't you join us for 8 and 9? That's all we're going to play, and then you can handle the back 9 on your own."

Jack pondered the proposition. Their applause sure felt invigorating, and maybe his game would benefit from a little support... at least for a couple of holes. "Sounds good," he replied.

John took the first turn, jumping with nervous energy as soon as he struck the ball, like he usually did. Jack always wondered how his friend was able to make his putts, but sure enough, the ball rolled smoothly into the hole. Bob missed his putt, though he seemed content with a 6. Harry fared no better than his companion.

That left Jack, who faced a five-foot putt that broke downhill and to the left. It occurred to him that he'd forgotten about the new USGA rule that you could leave the pin in when putting on the green. *A good time to utilize this option,* he thought. Jack didn't want to wind up short again, but if he hit the ball too hard, it could roll a fair distance past the hole. And his friends would all be watching.

He got himself set up and made contact. The ball had a good roll and turned left as he'd predicted. But then it passed the hole on the right side and stopped about ten inches beyond.

His three-man gallery let out a loud, "Ooooooooo," in unison. *This is like being in a professional tournament,* Jack noted. He tapped the ball in and allowed himself to be happy with a par.

John patted him on the back good-naturedly. On to number 8. With an entourage this time.

EIGHT

"Don't play too much golf. Two rounds a day are plenty."
Harry Vardon, British Professional Golfer

Number 8 at the Old Oak Country Club had similar statistics as the last hole: 345 yards with a par 4 and a handicap of 11. The fairway led straight uphill to an elevated green. Jack's friends urged him to take the first shot since he had the best score on number 7. Although Jack was anxious to prove that his performance hadn't been a fluke, he insisted on going last. He had just joined the group, after all, and he thought it made sense for them to stick to their regular order.

His buddies relented, and Bob went first. To no one's surprise, he had a slice, and the ball went swiftly out-of-bounds. *Nothing has changed with Bob,* Jack thought, bemused. The man kept an ample supply of golf balls in his cart out of necessity. Someday the pro shop would probably give him a plaque commemorating him as their number one ball customer.

Bob teed up a second time. This one veered to the right as well but managed to remain in play. Harry walked up to the tee next. He was the long hitter of the trio, and his ball took off to the left and landed in the rough. John had a good drive by his standards – straight, but only about 170 yards.

Now it was Jack's turn. As he drew his club from the bag, Jack realized he'd forgotten to review his performance on the last hole. *Maybe this is good,* Jack thought. Being with his buddies seemed to keep his mind in the present. When he first saw them on hole seven, he feared he would become a nervous wreck, overcome with the pressure of having to show off his new skills to his friends after declining to play with them for a full year. Instead, he felt oddly calm. *Whatever happens, happens,* he decided.

Following his pre-shot routine, Jack took his usual setup and swung away. The connection felt sound, and he noticed a slight increase in speed. The ball flew high, straight and long, sailing past Harry's ball and landing in the fairway.

Another round of applause erupted from his companions. "So, what's going on with your setup?" John asked. "You've got your clubhead a foot behind the ball."

"It's the single-plane way," Jack replied. "Moe Norman invented it."

"What good does that do?" muttered Bob.

"It helps you keep the club low to the ground for a head start on your turn."

Harry scratched his chin. "Why are your arms straight out, then?"

"That's so I can stay on the same plane," Jack responded. "I start out and finish in the same position."

"Is Moe the Canadian golfer who used a baseball grip?" Bob wanted to know.

"No, he used a palm-finger grip."

John and Harry attempted to mimic the maneuver for a few practice swings until Bob cleared his throat. "We oughta keep playing," he grumbled. "I've got places I need to be."

The trio's second shots were all fairly decent, but none of them made it to the green. They seemed more interested in observing Jack's next turn than in the quality of their own performance. Jack went last again because he'd had the longest drive – 250 yards, his best so far this morning. Although the pin stood 95 yards away, the distance would play like 110 yards because of the uphill slant. Normally, that would require a 9-iron, but with his increased speed, Jack thought his wedge would work just fine.

Jack was about ready to hit the ball when Bob shouted from across the fairway, "HOLD IT!" Bob and John came rushing over in their cart. Harry followed soon after.

"We wanted to be here for your next shot," John explained.

More pressure, Jack said to himself. Still, he vowed to play it just like his drive – without much deliberation. The pin was in the upper right corner where the green was more level, though it still sloped downward. He knew he needed to land beyond the pin; too close, and the ball could roll back off the green.

Harry asked, "Is the setup the same with an iron?"

Jack assured him it was. He demonstrated the single-plane swing one more time, and the ball traveled high, took a left turn toward the pin and landed a foot above and four feet to the right. More applause greeted his efforts. Jack wondered if he should have played the entire morning with his friends, but they probably couldn't have sustained this level of support for nine holes.

The other three took their third shots. Bob promptly lost his ball to the trap on the right. "My worst nightmare," he mumbled to himself. Harry had more success, landing thirty feet from the pin, and John made it to the fringe about the same distance away. Both seemed grateful to have just made it to the green.

Bob escaped his trap, only to land in another trap on the opposite side of the green. His fifth shot reached the green at last, and after two putts, he ended the hole with a 7. Harry and John finished with double bogies.

All eyes turned to Jack and his potential birdie. The putt would be from four feet away with a slight break to the left. He knew the speed of the ball was critical, and he would need to aim to the right to account for the break.

He tapped the ball. It had a good roll on the right line and started to turn left, but not enough to reach his target. The ball came to a stop one foot to the right of the hole. Another chorus of "Oooooo"'s arose from the spectators. Jack didn't mind; he was content to nudge the ball in for a par.

As they were heading for the next tee, Jack realized he'd been sensing discomfort from his friends. They'd been extremely friendly and supportive, so he couldn't figure out what was bothering them. Maybe they'd found out about his goal of scoring a sub-80 and were worried they were messing up his putts. Then it dawned on him: nobody had said anything yet about his birthday.

After they reassembled at the ninth tee, Jack asked casually, "I guess I'll see you all at the clubhouse later tonight, then?"

Relief spilled across his friends' faces. John confessed, "We didn't want to say anything. Bob thought it was some kind of surprise because your wife said to be at the Hogan Room no later than 6. She's never done anything like that before."

"She told me the same thing," Jack explained, "except to be there at 6:15, not before. She also ordered me to change my clothes in the locker room rather than come home. I'm in the dark as much as you guys."

Harry chimed in, "You'd better not be late, Jack. I'd hate to have to eat the birthday cake without you."

Bob shrugged. "More for us," he mumbled under his breath.

NINE

"When a round is going well and then turns sour, thoughts of the
past or future are usually the culprit."
Dr. Joe Parent, Author of *Zen Golf*

With a par of 4, the ninth hole had the distinction of being considered the most difficult segment of the entire course. Members feared it even more than the first hole, and it probably should have been assigned a handicap of 1 rather than 3. It sprawled across 400 yards and featured a slight bend to the right with an elevated green, while the Halfway House sat temptingly just beyond. Even if one had a successful drive of 200 yards, an equal amount of uphill distance remained... perhaps 175 yards, if one did well enough on the first shot.

Harry stepped up to the tee first, since he had a 5 on the last hole. He lived up to his reputation as the long driver of the group, sending his ball past the 200-yard marker but ending up in the left-side rough with no direct shot to the green. John had a straight drive, but it only went about 180 yards.

When it came to Bob's turn, the grim golfer stuck to his same pattern, starting things off with a slice out-of-bounds. It was as if he expected it, however; he immediately pulled a spare ball from the stockpile in his pockets and set it on the tee. This time, he hit a straight drive and landed not far from John's ball.

John patted him on the shoulder. "Always with the practice shot, eh, Bob?"

"Everyone has their routine," Harry quipped.

Jack was up next. He noticed that his wandering mind hadn't been a factor since joining this group. No more mental lessons; he just had to perform. All he wanted to do on this hole was hit straight for 180-200 yards, then make a shot of 120-150 yards so he could get close to the green. Attempting to reach the green on his second shot would pose a high degree of risk due to the out-of-bounds on the right side and the creek on the left.

He decided to use his fairway wood, which gave him a better chance of having a straight shot without depriving him of distance. Sure enough, his ball took off and landed a couple of yards beyond the 200-yard marker.

Bob walked up to him. "All right, Jack. Why are your feet so far apart when you set up?"

"It's for more stability," he replied.

"Fine, I can understand that... but your swing looks so strange."

Jack shrugged. "That's just what the single-plane swing looks like."

Bob seemed as if he were about to say something more, but he simply scratched his head and returned to his cart.

The four of them headed down the fairway for their second turns. Bob and John were the first to hit this time. As luck would have it, both their shots landed in the rough within a few feet of each other, 80 yards from the green and in playable terrain. Harry went next. His ball was potentially close enough to reach the green, so he made the gamble. His hit had enough distance, but the ball arced into the bunker on the left. At least that prevented it from rolling further into the creek.

When his turn came up, Jack used his wedge to get about 110 yards closer to the green. It was a little less than his desired distance, leaving him with 90 yards to go. Bob and John continued to make incremental progress with their third shots, although Bob's shot was technically his fourth, due to the penalty when his drive went out-of-bounds.

Jack, meanwhile, was itching to go again. He pulled his good old gap wedge out from his bag and eyeballed the remaining territory. The pin was right center this time, and he knew that if he aimed for the pin, his ball could roll back. To the right of the pin, the green was more level. That would be his target. He made good contact with his swing, but the ball landed on the right fringe about ten feet further than he had planned.

On the opposite side of the green, Harry just barely managed to get himself out of the trap, which left him with a thirty-foot putt. He pulled off a two-putt finish and scored a 5, as did John. Bob was laying 4, but he three-putted and ended up with a 7.

Now it was up to Jack. To make par, he would have to achieve a fifteen-foot putt, but he couldn't risk hitting the ball too hard. If he misjudged the shot, his ball could gain momentum on the downward slope and roll off the green entirely. *Better leave the pin in*, he decided. A safer strategy would be to nudge the ball gently downhill, then finish things with another putt to the left if the ball didn't go in.

As Jack stroked the ball, he felt a slight movement and stubbed his putter. The ball only rolled five feet. At least the remaining ten feet looked mostly level. He took a couple of steps around the hole just to make sure, then took his putt. To Jack's relief, and that of his friends, it went in. Five shots for this hole, which put him 4 over par for the course and gave him a tally of 39 for the front nine. 39 was better than 40, and more importantly, it meant that his goal of breaking 80 remained within reach.

On the drive up to the Halfway House, Jack critiqued his latest performance. His third shot had been offline, and he should have double-checked his alignment. He was well aware that he had moved during his first putt, *but why?* The most obvious answer was that he'd been thinking about whether or not he would stop for lunch. The smell of the Halfway House grill had a hypnotic effect on most players, and he was certainly not immune. *So much for staying in the present,* he thought.

Jack parked beside the building, but Bob and John pulled up alongside and remained in their seats.

"We *were* going to eat here," John explained, "but Bob wants a more substantial lunch back at the clubhouse."

"Burgers don't agree with my stomach," Bob added.

Jack turned down the offer to come join them. It wouldn't do to delay his game for an extended meal, and having a few minutes alone to consider the challenges ahead would probably improve his chances of breaking 80.

Harry caught up to them with his pull cart. "So, what did you shoot on the front nine?" he prodded.

Jack hesitated a bit too long. "I'll have to add it up. I wasn't really keeping track."

His old playing partners eyed him skeptically, but they let it slide. "You can let us know tonight," John offered, "and by the way, happy birthday from all of us. Good luck on the back nine!"

Harry crowded in with Bob and John, intending to tow his pull cart alongside their vehicle. When they drove away from the Halfway House, their passage stirred up the scent of sizzling meat from the grill. Jack decided he might as well treat himself to a light lunch. He'd earned it, if just barely. Whether he'd earn tonight's celebration after completing the back nine... that was yet to be determined.

INTERLUDE: THE HALFWAY HOUSE

"I'm still encouraged to go on. I wouldn't know where else to go."
E. B. White, American Writer

The Halfway House came across as a miniature version of the main clubhouse. The architecture and landscaping had been copied faithfully down to the ferns that framed the stone entranceway into the back patio. Jack strode through the passage and picked a table that overlooked the 9th hole.

Jack was pleased to see Mabel emerge from the building to take his order. She'd been running the Halfway House since long before Jack had joined the club. Over forty years now, he thought. The woman's specialty was a hamburger served on a hot dog bun and spiced with her own secret blend of seasonings. She kept these ingredients inside three large antique salt shakers, and she made sure to take them home with her every night. Due to these precautions, the clubhouse chef had been unable to duplicate the recipe, no matter how many times he tried.

Predictably, Jack ordered the hamburger with coleslaw. He hated to be so boring, but hopefully Mabel would take his consistency as a compliment. The community seemed to agree with his choices; several non-golfing members stopped by for lunch and takeout while he was waiting for his meal.

Just after his burger was served, the father and son duo that he'd seen at the first hole walked up and asked Jack if they could play through. He appreciated the courtesy and gave them the go-ahead. It would allow him time to analyze the front nine and think about the holes to come.

Jack knew he'd suffered some rough moments that morning, but he felt that he'd been able to course-correct and keep most of his errors from reoccurring. His main takeaway was that he needed to remember to do his practice swings. That way, he could settle into the moment and hit the ball without being distracted by thoughts. For the back nine, he could think of no better strategy. He just needed to trust in his swing.

Mabel stopped by to refill his water and leave the check. "Happy birthday, Mr. Santee," she said with a smile.

Jack was surprised. It was hard to keep secrets on club grounds, apparently. "How did you know?"

"I know most of the members' birthdays," she replied as she scooped up his empty plate. "And if I forget, it's right there on the manager's daily memo. I also noticed that Mrs. Santee is hosting your party in the Hogan Room."

That would explain it. "Well, thanks for lunch, Mabel," he said. "As long as there are empty tables out here, I'd like to wait a few minutes before heading to the 10th tee."

Mabel eyeballed him for a second. "You look like you're on some kind of quest, Mr. Santee. Relax awhile, and enjoy the back nine when you're ready."

"I will. Thanks again."

Jack had forgotten how good Mabel was at reading people. She had known the members longer than anyone and could always judge their moods and intentions. Her comment about his "quest" triggered a few questions in Jack's mind. What was so important about breaking 80, anyway? Did he want recognition at the club? A lot of the younger members shot in the 70s, and he knew a couple of golfers in their eighties who could break 80. He would certainly not be alone in his feat if he managed to do it.

The easier question in Jack's mind was: why do it on his 80th birthday? The answer tied back into his old career. When he worked in the advertising business, Jack had been the go-to person for catchy phrases and slogans. It was something he enjoyed and had an aptitude for, and that same instinct told him that that phrase "breaking 80 at 80" had some marketing potential. Maybe he could write a book with that title and share a little wisdom with his fellow golfers.

This rationale sounded logical to Jack, but he suspected his true motivation was simple: he was doing it for himself. If he was going to turn 80, he wanted the feeling of accomplishment of breaking 80 on the same day. He didn't need any other goal.

Still, a persistent thought tugged at his consciousness: what if he quit right now? He'd have a score of 39, which would be very respectable, given his age and handicap, and he'd avoid the risk of failing to break 80. But what would he do for the rest of the afternoon? Marie had ordered him to bring a change of clothes for the evening and to stay away from home.

If he didn't play the back nine, no one would know the difference, since he hadn't told a single person what he was trying to do. There were no words he needed to live up to... except for those that he had spoken to himself. That was the problem, really; he had never backed away from a personal challenge like this, and he didn't expect he would start now.

Jack signed the check, pushed his chair back and stood up. Nine down. Nine to go. And whatever happens, he'd be sure to find a lesson in it somewhere.

THE BACK NINE

TEN

"Take the risk or lose the chance."
Unknown

Back to the game.

After his extended lunch break at the Halfway House, Jack appreciated having hole number 10 to help him reorient toward the rigors of the back nine. It was only 335 yards to the pin with a handicap of 12 and a par of 4 – nothing that should tax his physical or mental faculties too harshly, at least in the beginning. His second shot would be tricky, though. The green had both a creek and a sand trap in front, plus another trap on the backside. Also, the green fell to the left; the only level spot was in the upper right corner. Targeting that specific patch of grass would be crucial.

First things first. Jack stepped up to the tee. He wouldn't need more than a 200-yard drive if he kept the ball on the left side of the fairway. If he succeeded, he would have a good angle up to the green.

After a few practice swings to knock the rust off, he went for it. The ball sailed all the way past the 200-yard marker and landed right on target. A good omen for how the back nine would play out, he thought. And hopefully, a good omen for how the "back nine" of his life would play out, too.

Today's game had conjured a great deal of introspection, Jack noticed. Perhaps he was getting too philosophical about everything. Or maybe he'd become delusional about the future; at eighty years old, he didn't really have a "back nine" ahead of him in terms of life expectancy. Probably not even a "back three". Nevertheless, Jack had maintained a "front nine" mentality for most of his life so far, all the way up to his eightieth birthday, and he didn't see much of an advantage in changing things up now. *I can always slow down once I'm dead,* he mused.

Jack's 205-yard drive had left him with 130 yards to the center of the green. The pin was in the right corner – a position often referred to as the "sucker pin location" by club members. If one aimed for the pin and failed to achieve a near-perfect shot, the trees along the right side of the fairway could intercept the ball and knock it off-course. Either that or the ball could roll off the backside and drop into the rear sand trap.

The shot with the greatest chance of success would require him to aim for the center of the green, even though the subsequent putt to the hole would not be easy. His 7-iron seemed like the right tool for the job – not too far and not too short. He took a practice swing and tried to focus. This was no time for lazy thinking, regardless of whether more blood was going to his digestive system than to his brain at that moment.

He swung. The ball struck the center of the green, bounced a couple of times, and came to a rest. For a second, Jack thought he saw the ball roll backward an inch, but to his relief, it held its position.

As Jack drove across the bridge to the green, his mind reflected upon the books he'd read about Moe Norman. Moe was the patron saint of the single-plane golf school Jack had attended earlier that year. Besides having invented the swing technique, the legendary golfer had a unique approach to putting. He didn't walk around the green to analyze the conditions; instead, he decided how the putt would go as he approached the green – just the opposite of what Jack had been doing. Jack didn't feel he had the expertise to read greens from afar. All the same, he tried not to spend too much time examining the green up close. Too often that led to second-guessing and faulty decisions.

Jack stepped out of his cart and lined up his putt. It appeared to be 15 feet and broke to the left, although due to the uphill, it would probably play more like 16 feet. He made sure to remain still, and he tried not to think about lunch, dinner, Moe Norman or anything else.

His putt had good contact; the ball made the full uphill distance, but it ended up rolling to the right and slightly past the hole. He was happy enough to tap it in for a par, since it was difficult to get down in two from where he had putted. Not a bad start for the back nine, and it kept his score at 4 over par, which was a relief.

Before heading to the next tee, Jack reviewed his performance once again. This had been a short hole, but all his hits had felt solid. He knew a great deal of his success was due to Moe's single-plane swing. He especially liked the simplicity of the backswing element; it was a two-piece move - straight back along the ground and then straight up.

Preoccupied with his thoughts, Jack had to abruptly swerve to avoid hitting the sign for the 11th tee. He glanced around to make sure no one had witnessed his gaffe. *Mental time's over,* Jack told himself. *Let's see what's next.*

ELEVEN

"A golf swing is a collection of corrected mistakes."
Carol Mann, American Professional Golfer

At 175 yards, hole number 11 was one of the shortest at Old Oak Country Club, even if the distance was considered dauntingly long for a par 3. Its difficulty was enhanced by an abundance of traps and a green that was challenging to come into. The handicap was 10.

Jack toyed with other options before selecting his 5-wood for the task. It would carry him to the front apron of the green; aiming any closer to the pin would be a risky move. If he tried, he was likely to end up in one of the traps *on eit*her side, or worse – he could get stuck behind the traps and be forced to vault his ball over them. In that scenario, he stood a high chance of overshooting his mark and rolling off the green into the opposite bunker. Far better to avoid that mess and land in front, for he felt he had the skills to finish the job in two.

He took some practice swings until he felt suitably centered, then made the shot. The ball flew straight across the fairway and landed right where he'd predicted. For a moment, Jack thought it might roll onto the green, but the ball stopped short. That was fine; he could still putt.

His next shot would be uphill with a slight turn to the left. Closing the 20-foot distance to the hole was important to Jack, so he accounted for the ascent in his calculations, and with every extraneous muscle held as still as possible, he made the putt. His ball reached the right elevation, but unfortunately, it didn't turn left as much as he'd predicted and he had to tap it in for a par. That was fine; hole 11 had always been a hard one for him, and he was still holding at 4 over par. Since Old Oak was a 70-par course, he had five strokes to spare in his quest to break 80.

Jack didn't think he had much to review this time – the hole had come and gone with tremendous speed – so his thoughts drifted back to Moe Norman and the golfer's famous swing technique. During single-plane school, Jack's instructor Danny Murphy frequently repeated Moe's belief that that the most important movement in the swing was the "vertical drop". Jack had known about this for years, but replicating the maneuver was easier said than done. He'd been able to imitate it in slow motion, but at full speed, he could seldom get his limbs to synchronize properly.

It wasn't until his time at single-plane school that he learned the importance of releasing his left knee toward the target, either on the downswing or sooner. He was also advised to simply forget about his arms; when he turned, they would drop correctly. After Danny showed Jack how to make these slight adjustments, everything clicked into place. The improvement to his game was immediate and, in Jack's mind, worth every penny. From that point onward, he focused on his legs and feet just as much as his arms and hands.

Lost in his memories again, Jack drove right past the 12th tee sign and had to turn around. At least he didn't nearly hit the sign with his cart like last time. While he backtracked, he noticed a car driving on an adjacent road that looked exactly like his son's new BMW X6. It obviously couldn't have been Jack, Jr., as his son had just called him this morning from his Northern California office to wish him a happy birthday. He thought it funny how whenever he or his son purchased a new vehicle, it always seemed unique during the first few days, but then his brain would start seeing the same car everywhere. *Maybe the model was trending,* he mused as he parked his cart at the 12th tee.

TWELVE

"I know I'm getting better at golf because I'm hitting fewer spectators."
Gerald Ford, 38th American President

This time, Jack was looking at a par 4, with a distance of 330 yards and a handicap of 16. *Should be an easy hole,* he thought, then immediately disavowed the sentiment. *There are no easy holes.*

The green was a straight shot from the tee box, but full of contours and hard to read, as he remembered. His driver would work fine to get him started, seeing that he had a wide enough fairway. He drew the club from his bag, but just as he was getting set up, Jack spied an approaching golf cart out of the corner of his eye. *That's odd.* He backed away from his ball and shaded his eyes. It didn't take him long to identify the driver; he recognized the sparkling white teeth of the man's smile before anything else.

Golf Pro Billy Matthews parked alongside the 12th tee and hopped out of his cart. He was in his late 30s and looked like the kind of person central casting would provide for a professional golfer in a golf movie. He never failed to wear the latest clothes from the pro shop, matched with a haircut straight out of the 1920s – combed back and parted in the middle. His chin appeared so clean and polished that Jack could have believed he'd shaved with a straight razor on the drive over.

Jack tapped his club against his shoe. "Hello, Billy. What's the occasion?" In the old days, if someone came out from the pro shop it was usually to deliver an emergency message. With the introduction of cell phones, that was no longer the case.

"Good afternoon, Mr. Santee. I just wanted to drive out to wish you a happy birthday. I'll be offsite by the time you come back in."

Jack shook his hand. "How did you know it was my birthday?"

"Mabel told me."

Of course, Jack thought.

"I know you have been working on the single-plane swing," Billy continued. "Would you mind if I follow you? Just for this hole?"

Jack knew there had to have been something else. *All I need is for the Pro to be watching me. Today of all days.* He held back a sigh. *Well, what's one more person,* he reasoned. *I did okay with my entourage before lunch, after all.* "Fine with me," he answered.

"Oh, great," said Billy. "The reason I asked was because we have an opening for a teaching pro, and I'm thinking about hiring someone with experience in single-plane swing technique. I've seen some videos, but I haven't been able to watch anyone in person who has taken up the swing."

Fair enough. Jack teed up again. He suddenly wished he could run through five or so of Danny Murphy's lessons, but he suppressed the urge. All he could do was hit the ball – a mantra that was beginning to sound very familiar by this point. He allowed himself a couple of practice swings, then took the shot. *Perfect contact.* His ball soared across the fairway, and Jack instantly knew he was looking at his best drive of the day.

"Wow," Billy murmured. "I had no idea you were striking the ball that well." He stepped out to the edge of the tee box. "I think you're close to the 250-yard marker."

Jack considered himself a humble man, but he couldn't keep a smile of pleasure from creeping onto his face.

Billy turned around. "I looked at your handicap before I came out. It's 17, and the last score you posted was an 89 one year ago. You're playing like a scratch golfer."

"I've only hit the ball once in front of you," Jack reminded him. "There's plenty more to go."

"Yes, maybe... but your swing looks very solid."

They drove out to Jack's ball and found it wasn't quite 250 yards. More like 245, which left Jack with a 110-yard approach shot. He decided to enlist his 9-iron. A wedge might have gotten him there, but the green was slightly elevated with the pin situated toward the upper left corner. That was the only level patch on the entire green. Any putt longer than fifteen feet would have to traverse some uneven terrain.

Billy judiciously withheld his advice and Jack didn't ask for any; he wanted to keep this an official round. After studying his options, Jack determined that if he targeted a spot pin high and just to the right of the hole, he would give himself the best chance of making the putt. After a set of practice swings, Jack swung once more, and the ball took off. It stayed right on line, landing pin high but just a bit more to the right than he'd wanted. Billy let out a low whistle, impressed.

When they arrived at the green, Jack found his ball lying twelve feet from the pin. The putt appeared level with a slight break on the right side of the hole. Billy looked over his shoulder and commented, "Nice approach."

True, Jack thought. The putt was level, but if he went long, the ball could easily roll several feet downhill. It seemed best to keep the ball on the left side of the hole and not let it go too far. If it somehow managed to drop in, so much the better.

His putt had a good roll, and it stopped short on the right side, allowing for an easy tap in. Jack was always glad to take "tap ins", especially when they were for par.

"You played that just right, Mr. Santee," declared the Golf Pro. "And after seeing your swing, I think I'll give serious thought to hiring a teacher with single-plane experience." Billy shook Jack's hand and added, "Congratulations on what you've accomplished, and best wishes again for a happy birthday." He climbed into his cart and waved goodbye, leaving Jack to continue on his own to the 13th hole.

THIRTEEN

"Success in golf depends less on strength of body than upon strength of mind and character."
Arnold Palmer, American Professional Golfer

On route to the 13th, Jack mused about the psychological aspects of golf. Mental discipline had become increasingly important to him in his later years, as evidenced by the large collection of self-help books he kept back in his study. Some volumes pertained to golf, like Dr. Mike's book, *Playing in the Now*. Others covered the gamut of inspirational topics such as everyday living, focusing on the present, goal-setting, visualization and positive thinking. Jack estimated he had over one hundred books in the self-help category, although several of them repeated each other's guidance, offering the same advice by way of different analogies.

He remembered reading the words spoken to Arnold Palmer by his father, "Golf is the only game played from the neck up."

Then of course there was Moe Norman's mantra, "Get out of your own way." After assimilating all of the recommendations, Jack had assembled his own pseudo-spiritual practice: picture the shot, acquire the right feeling with a practice swing, then take the shot without any further thought. He figured that with a blank mind, the only place he could be was in the present.

Jack reached the 13th tee and saw the route was all clear. The hole was 400 yards – a par 4 with a handicap of 6. Several trees hung over the left side of the fairway about 150 yards distant, while a pair of traps lay in wait on the opposite side. In the past, Jack's plan would have been to take three shots to reach the green, then hope for a single putt to achieve a par. A bogey would also be acceptable, especially on a 6-handicap hole. But now he was consistently hitting the ball further; with a good drive, he could end up 150 yards out instead of his usual 200, setting himself up to reach the green on his second shot. *Well, I won't lose anything by trying,* Jack reasoned.

He kept to his mental routine and sure enough, his drive took off, sailing far past the 200-yard marker. The shot landed 230 yards out, leaving him with 170 yards to the green. After catching up to his ball, Jack looked back and noticed he had cleared the overhanging trees on the left side of the fairway by only three or four feet. *That was lucky.*

The green lay straight ahead, but it was well-trapped on both the left and the right. In addition, a grass trap sat directly in front. Jack could never remember the name of the grass, but he knew it was tough material and could easily snare his club head if he needed to fight his way out.

Rather than aim for the green, Jack supposed he could also lay up and position himself 50 yards from the hole using his 60-degree wedge. His chances of getting a par would be very poor using that strategy, but at least he wouldn't get tangled up in the grass trap. Most likely he would end up with a bogey or double bogey.

Too much analysis, Jack thought. *Just go for the green... you're hitting the ball well enough to do it.* His 5-wood felt perfectly designed for the task; he could aim to the left, avoid the trap and still get on the green in two shots.

He swung. The ball took off with good contact and seemed destined for the green. But as he watched, the ball angled slightly to the right and disappeared into the grass trap. Jack shook his head. *Did I talk myself into that result?* He didn't regret taking the risk because he'd been striking the ball so well. But now he was forced to extricate himself from a difficult trap.

His 64-degree wedge would be the best club for this grass trap shot. That particular club was unheard of when he first started playing golf; he could only remember the sand wedge being used, and it took many years for the other variants to come along. These days, however, it wouldn't be unusual to find three or four wedges in every golf bag. *He* certainly wouldn't consider playing the game without them.

Jack had been introduced to the 64-degree wedge after being told he couldn't attend a short game school without one. Apparently, he'd been a late adopter. The club was good for 10-30 yards and always produced a high shot. That seemed useful since he had 20 yards left to the pin at the back of the green. He would have to have a strong follow-through, however, if he wanted to avoid any entanglement with the grass.

Jack continued to make good contact with the ball. It landed to the left of the pin, about twelve feet out – further away than he'd planned. Jack bit his lip. The chances of making par now seemed rather slim.

His putt had a break to the right, and it looked important to stay above the hole this time; if he were short, his ball could take a sharp right turn and roll further downhill than the point from where he'd started. Jack held still and steady as he made the putt. The ball had a good roll, but it stopped to the left, hole high and about eighteen inches out.

Thankfully, Jack was able to make the final putt, giving him a 5 for the hole. He was now 5 over par with 5 holes to go. *That's too many fives,* he thought. *I don't need any more fives unless it's on a par 5.* Although he felt okay with a bogey on a 6-handicap hole and he knew he could get a birdie on one of the remaining holes, he couldn't help but feel a little more anxious than he had just ten minutes ago.

Stay sharp, Jack, he advised himself. *Things could get trickier from here.*

FOURTEEN

*"You don't know what pressure is until you play for five bucks
with only two bucks in your pocket."*
Lee Trevino, American Professional Golfer

As he pulled up to the 14th hole, Jack realized that his margin for error was beginning to look fairly slim. At this point in the game, he could only spare four shots over par and still break 80. This hole could be an opportunity to add a fifth extra shot to his reserves, however. It was a par 4 with a 14 handicap and was considered one of the easier stretches on the course at 280 yards. The word "easier" didn't linger in Jack's thoughts for once.

The fairway appeared straight, with traps to the left and right about 200 yards out. Jack got himself in position, intending to hit one right down the middle just in case his ball couldn't muster more than 200 yards. Then he saw yet another golf cart headed in his direction.

Jack sighed. *Might as well have the whole club out here.*

When the cart drew closer, Jack identified the driver as Tim Smith, the golf course superintendent. Tim had been around nearly as long as Mabel. He kept the Old Oak course in perfect shape, as evidenced by the numerous awards he'd received from the superintendent's association, and he was one of the first greenskeepers in the country to receive a bachelor's degree in Golf Turf Management. Some would say that he had the complete opposite fashion sense from slick Golf Pro Billy Matthews; Tim dressed like a "grass farmer" – a humble epithet that he often used to describe himself – and he only shed his workman's garb when he played golf with his 6 handicap.

Tim parked his cart and approached the tee box. "Hi there, Mr. Santee. I came out to wish you a happy birthday before I left for the day."

"Thanks, Tim," said Jack. "Mabel told you?"

"No, the Pro did, actually. He also said that if I wanted to see a single-plane swing, I should head down here. I've been curious about it for some time. Of course, I don't want to interrupt your game... I'll just watch a couple of shots, and then I need to go check out the 14th green."

Here we go again, Jack thought. *Another gallery.* His irritation was tempered by the fact that thus far, his audiences hadn't affected his game. "No problem, Tim," he told him.

Sure enough, Jack managed to hit a perfect drive between the two traps. Tim was impressed.

"Great contact! Your swing looks just like I've seen in videos. I didn't realize there was a wide stance involved, though. And I noticed you set the club back a foot from the ball."

"I did," Jack replied. "That's the way Moe Norman did it, and it worked well for him. But you're a 6 handicapper, Tim... I don't know if you need to change anything."

The look on Tim's face said otherwise. "I've been stuck at a 6 for years and I can't seem to improve. I need to do something different. Let me watch you hit one more time, and then I'll meet you up at the green."

Jack relocated for his second shot. He was now 80 yards from the green, but he needed to aim for 90 yards in order to reach the pin in back. He considered his gap wedge but didn't think it would get him far enough; the pitching wedge felt more suitable. Tim waited on the cart path nearby, anxious to see how he'd do.

Jack cleared his mind and swung. His ball arced over the fairway and landed six feet above and to the left of the pin. Tim applauded heartily, then continued down the path.

When Jack reached the green, he found the superintendent walking around the hole with his putter and a ball, checking the conditions. The man stepped aside and waited for Jack to make his move.

The six-foot putt looked straight but downhill. *Another good time to leave the pin in.* Jack had a feeling it might be fast because the grass around the hole appeared shorter than usual. A half-length putt sounded just about right. He took the shot, and his ball remained right on line up until the moment where it hit the pin and rolled a foot beyond the hole. Another tap in, and unfortunately, it wasn't the birdie he'd had planned. At least he didn't lose anything to par this time.

"Well done," Tim commented. "Thanks for letting me watch a couple of shots. I noticed that even when putting, you extend your arms while still staying over the ball." He mimed the position to see how it felt. "*Hmmmm.* You've got me interested in that swing of yours. Billy says he's thinking about hiring a single-plane instructor."

"That's what he told me," Jack responded. "By the way, what were you checking on the green?"

Tim glanced back at the hole. "Oh, I had couple complaints today about this green being too fast. I didn't want to say anything earlier as I thought you wouldn't want any inside information that would give you an advantage for your round."

"I appreciate that."

"Well, usually when I get these complaints, it turns out the cause is poor putting. In this case, I did find the grass had been cut too short and rolled too much."

Jack nodded. "That's what I saw, too, except it was even faster than I guessed."

"I'll see you around the Club, then." Tim shook his hand firmly. "Wishing you lots of pars and birdies for the rest of your round, Mr. Santee."

The greenskeeper waved goodbye, leaving Jack to venture on to the 15th tee in good spirits.

FIFTEEN

"The most dangerous time when the cords of concentration are most apt to snap is when everything is going smoothly."
Bobby Jones, American Amateur Golfer

Jack had the sensation of being on "cruise control". After fourteen holes, he had stopped having thoughts about the mechanics of his swing and body stance. He no longer needed to run golf school lessons through his mind before every shot, and the experience felt enormously liberating. Back on the 12th, Billy had told him that his swing looked very solid. *This might be my day after all,* Jack thought. *I just have to stick to my routine.*

The 15th hole was a 400-yard, par 4 situation with a 2 handicap – the second-hardest hole at Old Oak. Achieving a par at this difficulty level would be outstanding. The green was a straight shot from the tee, and the only trap in between lay about 225 yards along the right side of the fairway. He expected he was unlikely to reach the trap, but if his ball came anywhere close, it would help that the fairway sloped away from it.

Jack's drive landed just left of the trap and proceeded to roll into the center of the fairway. A 225-yard drive was unexpected, but the Pro *had* mentioned he was swinging well. Another 175 yards would get him to the green, where the pin stood directly in the center.

Jack had no doubt that he could get there on his next stroke, but any miscalculation would unleash a load of trouble. Three traps surrounded the green, including directly in front. The left trap bordered a creek and beyond the right trap was out-of-bounds. On top of all that, the green itself was elevated and full of waves. No one could say that the hole's handicap of 2 was unearned.

Jack puzzled over his strategy for a while. One option involved hitting a 100-yard shot, followed by a 75-yard contribution by his trusty gap wedge. That would bring the ball close enough for him to wrap things up with a putt for par. Or instead, he could use one of his favorite clubs, the 5-wood, to get the ball on the green, leaving him with two putts to make par.

Despite his undeniable progress over the last year, Jack still couldn't shake the mentality of a 17-handicapper. Going straight for the green felt too risky. He selected his wedge and took the shorter shot. It went flawlessly. His ball landed 80 yards from the pin, right below the green and its closest bunker.

Jack felt completely relaxed as he pulled his gap wedge from his bag. *This is like catching fish in a barrel.* He had made this shot countless times and almost always came close to his intended target. Without another thought, he got set up and gave himself permission to swing away. Immediately, Jack heard the sound no golfer wants to hear: the unmistakable *clunk* of a shanked shot. The ball took a hard right turn and flew out-of-bounds.

Jack was stunned. "Where did *that* come from?" he asked aloud. A cascade of judgments crashed through his brain. *I'm a fool. I've lost all chance of breaking 80 just because of a single shot. I've used up too many strokes. What an idiot I was to think I could break 80 with a 17 handicap when I'm such a sporadic player. Thank God I didn't tell anyone what I was trying to do today. If I'd had any sense, I would have quit after the first 9.*

The incriminations piled up fast and thick, but Jack finally drew a long breath and gave himself a minute to calm down. He decided that he needed to just keep playing, even if the goal of breaking 80 had very likely drifted beyond his reach. He dropped another ball onto the grass.

Unfortunately, Jack now felt completely confused about what to do next. He certainly didn't want another shank, but he didn't know what he could do differently, either. Perhaps it had been a fluke. He decided to trust in his process and forgo the analysis for now. With another good hit, maybe he could regain a sliver of his confidence.

He tried another shot. No shank this time, but the ball arced to the left and landed in the left bunker. Jack was now laying 5 with a penalty shot. He made it out of the trap successfully without showering the green with too much sand, and the ball came to rest fifteen feet from the pin. *Thank god*, he thought. *Another shank would have killed me.*

Now he was laying 6 with a tricky putt – downhill, with a break to the left about a foot out. Jack left the pin in. He tried to focus on the present and get the bad shot out of his mind as he walked around and observed the terrain from other angles. His initial read seemed to be correct. Jack set himself up. *Here goes. Do or die.*

To his immense surprise, the ball went in. Scoring a 7 on a par 4 was a rather dubious victory, of course. Now he could add a 3 to his already-5-over-par, making it 8 over. *Talk about snatching defeat from the jaws of victory,* he thought, wincing. Three holes remained, and he could only spare a single shot over par while still breaking 80. *That shot had better not be a shank,* Jack declared to himself. He got in his cart and drove off to the 16th tee, determined to figure out what had gone wrong.

SIXTEEN

"Of all the hazards, fear is the worst."
Sam Snead, American Professional Golfer

The moment Jack stepped foot on the 16th tee box, he pulled out his gap wedge and started swinging away, trying to figure out what had gone wrong. He couldn't remember the last time he had shanked a shot. The textbook reason for his mistake was simple: golfers sometimes got outside on the downswing and had to cut across to get back to the ball, which then caused them to make contact with the hosel or the heel of the club. *But why did I get outside?*

He took a couple more swings. Something didn't feel right. Then it finally clicked – he wasn't turning his lower body toward the target before he started his downswing. He'd failed to do the "vertical drop", which admittedly was a common failing of his when he became too tired. Jack kicked himself for not realizing what was happening. He'd have to focus more on

his mechanics during the last three holes, which could be prob-
lematic if he was simultaneously trying to maintain a blank
mind and feel the swing. *Well,* Jack thought, *if I'm going to ever
integrate all these disciplines, now is the time to do it.*

Absorbed in his exercises, Jack failed to observe that he had
caught up with the father and son team that he had let play
through at lunchtime. He only spotted the duo as they walked
onto the green, 150 yards away, but they noticed him immediately afterward and waved for him to take his shot.

Here we go again, Jack grumbled to himself. *Another audience.*
Focusing on his swing would be that much harder.

The 16th was a par 3 with a handicap of 18. Measurably easy,
yet he faced this hole with trepidation. *What's next... a slice?
Maybe a hook?* Thankfully, a simple quote from Moe Norman
popped into his head: "Bad thinking, bad golf. Good thinking,
good golf." Jack removed his cap and ran a hand through his
thinning white hair. *Guess I'd better choose "good",* he told
himself.

He decided he could reorient his mind by focusing on the hole's
physical conditions. On the far side of the fairway and directly
in front of the well-trapped green, a ravine yawned hungrily. If
he wanted to make par, then the only sensible way to reach the
pin was to carry the full 150-yard distance, ravine and all. With
the high likelihood of incurring penalty shots on this hole, Jack
knew he had little margin for error. At least the pin was set
back, which would allow for some roll to occur and be
beneficial.

Jack belatedly waved to the twosome to acknowledge their offer.
Then he took a couple of swings to make sure he was turning
correctly. He planned on taking plenty of club with his 7-wood

on this shot.

When he connected, everything felt good. His ball landed on the green, but because the pin stood behind a slight hill, he couldn't tell if he'd gone long or not. The ball could have rolled off the backside, and the lack of applause from his new audience meant he couldn't discount that possibility quite yet.

The father and son duo greeted him as soon as he arrived at the green. Jack had met the dad previously, but he couldn't remember his name; the man was a newer member. Thankfully, he didn't have to guess for long.

"Good afternoon, Jack." The older man shook Jack's hand. "Winston Wakefield. And this is my son, Tommy. We've met before. I believe you knew my father, Alfred, back in New York?"

"Ah, yes," Jack replied. "Thanks for reminding me."

Winston beamed at him. "That was a great shot. I knew you were a legend in the advertising business, but I didn't know you were such a good golfer."

Jack shrugged, embarrassed. "I didn't even see where my ball went."

Winston pointed. "It's right over there, three feet from the pin."

Sure enough, there it was. Jack breathed a sigh of relief. "Thanks. A lucky shot, I guess."

Jack's comment earned a skeptical look from Winston. "I'm a new golfer," he said, "but that seemed like more than luck."

Tommy and Winston were further back, so they putted first. They both missed the hole but made their second putts. Jack's turn was next. Since his previous shot, a degree of confidence had returned to him. *Maybe I need a gallery of spectators after all.*

He examined the terrain. The three feet between his ball and the hole looked straight and level, but he didn't want to come up short. He took a slow breath and made the putt. The ball took a beeline for the hole... then abruptly lipped out.

Tommy groaned in sympathy. "You were robbed!"

"I hit it a little too hard," Jack admitted. He made the tap in and was thankful for a par after the shocking disappointment of the last hole.

Winston assumed the senior golfer would want to play on through, but Jack had another idea. "Why don't we play the last two holes together?" Jack suggested.

The father glanced aside at Tommy. "We wouldn't want to interfere with your game. Neither of us are very good."

"It's no problem," Jack reassured him. And he meant it. In a complete reverse of his earlier thinking, Jack decided that he liked having company after all. More importantly, his game didn't seem to mind.

As Jack drove behind the new club members toward the 17th tee, he studied Tommy a little. The boy looked to be about twelve – the same age Jack was when he first started playing with his dad. *Full circle,* he thought. How many generations had carted their clubs across these hills, Jack wondered, passing the rituals of this sport from father to son? Standing next to these two, he couldn't help but feel a little old, but also connected to something timeless. Maybe he'd manage to pass on something worthwhile today... some bit of wisdom that would be carried and translated through the ages into one form or another.

Lofty thoughts for an old golfer, he chided himself. Still, you never knew when you might have an impact on a person.

SEVENTEEN

"When I play my best golf, I feel as if I'm in a fog, standing back watching the earth in orbit with a golf club in my hands."
Mickey Wright, American Professional Golfer

The three of them reconvened at the 17th tee. This hole was 380 yards and had a 4 for both par and handicap. With that kind of distance, beating par would not be easy.

"Par shooters go first," Winston directed.

Jack preferred to play last, but he acquiesced and drew his club from his bag. After going through his usual motions, he hit a straight drive of about 225 yards. Not a bad start, he thought.

Winston went next and sliced his drive about 160 yards, though it looked playable from the rough. Tommy geared up for his turn, but instead of teeing up his ball, the boy approached Jack and said, "I'd like to try your swing, Mr. Santee. Could you show me?"

Jack took a breath and considered. "Maybe we could go to the practice range next week. During a game is not the best time to learn a new swing."

"It's okay," Tommy reassured him. "This is just a practice round for my dad and me."

Winston spoke up. "Not a good idea, Tommy. We're already intruding on Mr. Santee."

Tommy looked disappointed as he walked to the tee, and Jack reconsidered. *Kids need a lot of support at that age,* he remembered. *I certainly did.* "Tommy, I'd be glad to help." Jack retrieved his club and joined the boy. He modeled the correct positioning, saying, "Just get lined up, extend your arms and hold a wider stance. Then take the club back along the ground as you begin your backswing."

Tommy watched him carefully and tried to mimic his movements. On his first swing, however, the boy barely made contact. The ball landed just past the lady's tee.

"That's enough, Tommy," his father said brusquely. "We need to move on."

"Let me try another one," the boy pleaded. "Mr. Santee, could you show me the setup again?"

Jack took a glance at Winston and decided the father was just trying to be polite. He talked Tommy through the technique one more time and let the boy watch some additional practice swings. Tommy studied his movements closely, and then he made a second attempt. This time, the boy had a solid hit of about 180 yards, straight down the middle.

"Wow," said his dad, awestruck. "Where did that come from? Tommy's been hitting his drives about 150 yards, and not usually that straight."

Jack shrugged. "Kids learn fast. The swing is fairly simple, too. It's called the single-plane swing."

"I could use a bit of that," Winston admitted.

Tommy walked up to Jack and asked, "Can I ride the rest of the way with you?"

Jack wasn't exactly looking for a sidekick. Still, he found himself saying, "Yes, you can... but ask your dad first."

Winston gave his permission. "Actually," the father added, "I think I'll just observe you two playing these last two holes. No need for me to finish. I'd like to try to learn more about this swing of yours."

Tommy transferred his clubs to Jack's cart - an unnecessary move, but Jack didn't protest. Then they drove down the fairway with Tommy's dad following close behind.

Jack felt somewhat mystified at how this game had progressed. He thought he would have been playing alone for eighteen holes, but so far, he'd been joined by his old golf partners, the pro, the greenskeeper and now a father and son duo. In addition to all that weirdness, Jack had suddenly become a golf instructor. *What an odd round this has turned out to be.*

Lost in his thoughts, Jack momentarily also lost track of where he stood with the score. *That's probably not a bad thing,* he conceded. It wouldn't help to dwell on the fact that he was 8 over par with only one shot to spare if he wanted to break 80. On the positive side, his swing felt sound again, but he knew he would have to remain diligent after the disaster on the 15th hole.

He cast those thoughts from his mind as they parked and caught up to the twelve-year-old's ball. "Looks like you have a good lie, Tommy," Jack observed. "What club are you going to use for this one?"

"I was thinking about my 5-iron. I usually hit well with that."

Jack nodded. "Just keep it to the right, and you'll have a good angle to the hole."

Tommy got into position. "Does my setup look right?"

"Looks fine to me."

The boy's shot went about 120 yards and landed close to where Jack had suggested, leaving him with a 100-yard shot to reach the green. Winston watched from off to the side and made no comment.

For his second shot, Jack was looking at a 175-yard distance from his position on the right side of the fairway. The angle was good; he expected he could reach the green with his fairway wood, but the target was surrounded by traps and he feared he might easily end up in one of them.

He pulled his 5-wood from his bag and took a couple of practice swings. The grass in front of the green had plenty of space for a safe landing, and that's where he aimed. To Jack's relief, his ball appeared to touch down right where he needed it to land, but he would have to wait for Tommy's third shot before he could verify his success.

The boy had 100 yards remaining, and after asking Jack's advice, he decided to use his 7-iron. He landed short of the green, but within putting or chipping distance.

Jack approached his ball and liked what he saw. 50 yards to go. He drew his own 7-iron, aimed carefully, and his chip shot ended up left of the pin by about four feet. Tommy followed, making a nearly identical chip shot that came to rest five feet below the pin. The boy's putt fell short, but he made the next one, earning him a 6 on his second ball. "That's the best score I've ever had on this hole!" Tommy crowed.

Jack examined his four-foot putt carefully. It appeared to break to the right, but not by much, and it looked about a hole out to the left. He took a couple of practice swings, and when he made contact, his ball had a good roll but slowed down and turned right too soon. He had to tap it in again, giving him a 5 for the hole and 9 over par for the course.

He sighed. *I was only one shot better on that hole than my new twelve-year-old student,* Jack thought. *There's something wrong with this picture.* He shook his head in an attempt to clear it. There would be plenty of time for such thoughts later this evening. For now, he needed to focus on the final hole. He now had exactly zero strokes to spare if he was going to break 80.

The group met up at their golf carts. Winston congratulated his son, then asked Jack how he'd learned about the single-plane maneuver.

"Oh, a while back, I read about a Canadian professional golfer by the name of Moe Norman who invented the swing," Jack explained. "I'd always been interested in it, but I didn't pursue any instruction until the last couple of years. You can watch some videos online about it before you consider taking lessons."

"Nice. I think I'll need an edge if I want to keep up with Tommy, here." He gave his son a friendly pat on the back.

And with that, they were off to the 18th and final hole.

EIGHTEEN

"It ain't over till it's over."
Yogi Berra, American Baseball Player and Manager

As they drove toward the last tee, questions came spilling out of Tommy as fast as his mentor could answer them, but Jack discovered that he really didn't mind. He wasn't sure if the boy reminded him of himself at that age or if he was simply being reminded of times spent with his own son on a golf course.

Whatever it was, the interaction gave Jack a peaceful feeling – a welcome contrast to all the ups and downs of the day. He realized that as wonderful as breaking 80 would be, a score of 80 or 81 would be very respectable, especially for someone his age whose last handicap was a 17. He'd be content with any score in the low 80s, really. Breaking 80 could always wait for another day; an afternoon next week or next month would work just as well as his actual birthday.

Jack realized he was probably just cushioning the disappointment of missing his goal with these thoughts. He decided to confide in the twelve-year-old. "Tommy, can you keep a secret?"

"Sure thing, Mr. Santee." The boy leaned in close, wide-eyed, as if Jack were about to reveal the mysteries of the golfing universe.

"Today is my 80th birthday... and I'm trying to break 80."

"That's great!" Tommy cheered. "What's your score now?"

Jack hated to discourage the kid, but it didn't seem fair to get his hopes up. "I'm at 74 so far, so I'll need to get a 5 on this hole to break 80. I'd really like to, but if it doesn't happen, it'll be fine. The most important part of today is the birthday party my wife is throwing for me back at the clubhouse."

"You can do it if you want to," Tommy insisted.

Jack smiled. "Good thought, Tommy. Thanks."

They parked at the 18th tee and assessed the final hole. It was a par 5 with 490 yards of distance and a handicap of 8. The layout was simply stunning. Its fairway sloped upwards to reach the green, and the clubhouse, framed by mountains, created an elegant backdrop behind it. This was the longest hole at Old Oak, and the steady uphill grade guaranteed it would be anything but easy. Still, Jack considered the 18th to be a fair challenge and a suitably-designed conclusion to a classic course.

Jack offered to go first this time, mostly for Tommy's benefit so the boy could observe what the swing looked like again. He noted a trap on the left side of the fairway, but it appeared hard enough to reach that it wouldn't be a concern. *This is my final drive,* he thought. *I need to make it a good one.*

Thankfully, Jack made what he guessed was his best contact of the day. It could have been a 250-drive, were it not for the uphill slant of the fairway. As it was, his ball stopped just past the 200-yard marker. Jack wasn't disappointed, though. He had hit it solid and, most importantly, straight.

Tommy was itching to take his turn. His practice swings had begun to look remarkably similar to Jack's own. When the boy hit, it was a straight shot across the fairway. His ball might have traveled 180 yards, but the gradient kept it from going more than 160.

Winston had remained quiet up until this point; now he applauded heartily. "A good shot, Tommy," he commended. "You're lucky to be playing with Mr. Santee today."

"He's got talent, Winston," Jack agreed. "All Tommy needed was to see the swing."

The boy used his fairway wood for his second shot, and it went 150 yards and straight.

Jack complimented Tommy on his consistency as he stepped up for his turn. He expected he could get within 130 yards of the green with his seven wood. "I need to hit far enough so I can use my 8 or 9-iron next," he explained to his student.

"You can do it, Mr. Santee."

Who's coaching who now? Jack wondered, but he thanked the boy for his encouragement. He then lived up to expectations by hitting another shot straight up the fairway that placed his ball within 120 yards of the green.

"I *knew* you could do it!" Tommy cheered.

The boy got ready for his third shot. He used his 5-wood this time, and although the ball went only about 130 yards, it flew straight. On his fourth turn, he would only need to make an additional 50.

Jack faced a 120-yard distance for his own third shot, but the green was elevated enough that he'd have to tack on an extra 5-10 yards to compensate. He would also need to carry the green to avoid the trap in front and reach the pin, which stood in the back. *It had to be playing 130 yards,* he estimated. An 8-iron might work, but he remembered how many times he had wound up in the front trap on his hole. His 7-iron seemed a safer bet.

"It's do-or-die time, Tommy," he announced. "I have to get on the green and be close enough for at least a two-putt to make par."

"You can do it again," Tommy insisted. "I know you can."

Those words did well to buttress Jack's spirits. He tried to focus his positive energies on the outcome and swung away. The ball arced over the trap and remained centered on the pin, but unfortunately, it bounced and rolled past his target about ten additional feet, stopping right up against the back fringe.

"See, I *told* you!" Tommy said smugly.

"Thanks," said Jack, "but I was hoping not to be that far back with a downhill putt."

"Yeah, but you're putting for a birdie, Mr. Santee."

Jack admitted he should be thankful for that. He had two chances to get par and break 80, but the downhill putt meant that he still stood a real chance of messing things up.

Tommy's fourth shot needed to travel 50 yards to reach the green, or 60 to reach the pin in the back. The boy used his sand wedge and just barely cleared the front trap, landing on the fringe. He recovered by chipping his ball with the 7-iron and it came to rest one foot from the pin, in front of Jack's.

"Go ahead," Jack urged, "hit it in for your 6."

Sure enough, the putt went in. Tommy was thrilled. "I got the best score I've ever had on this hole, too! Can't thank you enough, Mr. Santee."

Jack smiled back at him. "You're welcome, Tommy. I think we've helped each other."

Now came the putt of Jack's life. *Okay, not exactly,* he thought. It would have felt that momentous if he'd kept the attitude he had at the start of the round, hours earlier. But at this point, he was just enjoying the day.

Tommy came over to stand beside him, while Winston watched from the side of the green, unaware of Jack's 80th birthday ambitions. "It's going to be fast," Jack explained to the boy. "Looks like twelve feet. I can't be long, or it's going to roll off the green." *If there was ever a time to leave the pin in, it was now,* Jack thought.

Tommy looked up at him questioningly. "Would it be better not to think about it? About it rolling off, I mean."

The kid's a zen master, too. "You're right, Tommy. I've spent this whole round trying to stay positive. That's more important now than ever."

"Just get it close. Close and safe."

"All right, then," Jack agreed. "It's another do-or-die."

Even that thought seemed more dramatic than necessary. He took a deep breath, cleared his head and gave himself a moment to enjoy the space it opened up within his mind. It felt good.

Jack barely touched the ball, but it went rolling fast. For a second, he feared it would be impossible for friction to slow the ball down in time. *Five feet... four feet... three... two... one...* Then it came to rest... two inches from the hole. A tap in.

Tommy whooped and jumped into the air. "You did it, Mr. Santee! Congratulations!" He took the pin out for Jack and held up his hand for a high-five.

Jack returned the gesture, then strode over and nudged his ball into the cup. *Well, I'll be darned. 79. It really happened.*

Winston came onto the green. "What's all the excitement about?"

"Can I tell my dad?" Tommy asked.

Jack plucked his ball from the hole and shrugged. "I guess so, Tommy. It's no big deal."

The boy grinned at being able to share their secret. "Mr. Santee shot a 79 on his 80th birthday, dad!"

Winston's eyes widened. "Well, that's great, Jack! Happy birthday, and thanks so much for helping Tommy. He's really improved in just two holes, and I learned a lot myself. I definitely want to work on mastering that single-plane swing." He helped Tommy retrieve his clubs from Jack's cart, then gave Jack a handshake along with his best wishes for the evening. Tommy was content to say farewell with another high-five.

Jack was almost sorry to see them leave. He admitted that it felt nice to have someone share in his victory. *I guess contemplative time is nice, too.*

He stowed away his putter and rested behind the wheel of the golf cart for a few minutes. Jack expected to feel differently. After all, this had been the culmination of... well, not his life or career or anything, but certainly of all the hard work he'd put in over the last few years. His triumph must not have sunken in quite yet. *But if I don't end up feeling any different by tomorrow, does that even matter?*

Jack assumed there probably was a quote from one of the golf legends that could effectively sum up moments like these. Maybe someone in the pro shop could provide him with one. He needed to head over there to turn in his score anyway.

And with that thought, Jack got behind the wheel of his cart and left the course behind him.

CHAPTER 19: THE CLUB ROOM

"I never played a round when I didn't learn something new about the game."
Ben Hogan, American Professional Golfer

Jack walked into the pro shop to turn in his score. The assistant behind the counter, Mike, sat up and gave him a nod of acknowledgment. Mike's military crew cut and regulation mustache made him look gruffer than Jack knew him to be.

"How was your round, Mr. Santee? Happy birthday, too, by the way."

"Thank you, Mike." Jack had meant to keep his accomplishment mostly to himself, but he found himself saying, "I did manage to break 80 with a 79."

Mike slapped the counter. "Fabulous!"

As Jack pulled up his account on the pro shop computer, Mike leaned over and glanced at the screen. "I see you got an 89 a year ago; that's quite an improvement." The assistant scratched his chin. "Breaking 80 on your 80th birthday... might be a title for a book."

Jack was glad someone else had thought about a similar name. "It has a good ring to it," he agreed as he typed in his score.

Mike made eye contact with a skinny, younger attendant, who left the shop in a hurry. At the risk of sounding nosy, Jack asked, "Where's your helper going in such a rush?"

Suddenly, the assistant's gruffness seemed genuine. "He's late for an appointment," was all Mike would tell him.

Jack glanced at his watch and saw it was nearly 5 o'clock. An hour and fifteen minutes until the party. He decided to say goodbye and head for the men's locker room where the Club Room was located. The day had left him emotionally exhausted. He didn't know whether he needed soda, coffee or a healthy dose of alcohol. Perhaps all three. He'd figure it out when he got there.

Jack entered the Club Room and quickly spotted Oscar Jackson polishing glasses with a rag behind the bar. Oscar managed the employees working on his side of the clubhouse, including the bar and the locker room. Like Mabel, he had worked at Old Oak for about forty years, and he possessed a similar encyclopedic knowledge of every club member. He read Jack's demeanor instantly.

"You look beat up, Mr. Santee," said Oscar. He set down a glass and tucked the rag into his belt. "What can I fix you for your birthday? It's on the house."

Behind the bar, Jack noticed a copy of the manager's memo that listed his name. "That's good of you, Oscar. I'll have a light gin and tonic. Going to a party at 6:15."

"Hogan Room, right? I hear your wife's been working hard to put this one together. You're a lucky man, Mr. Santee."

There are no secrets in this club, Jack thought to himself. *At least I can decide who I want to tell about my score.*

Oscar delivered his drink with a smile. "You'll feel better after one of these. Bet you used up a lot of energy breaking 80 today."

Jack nearly spit out his first sip. "How did you know?"

Oscar shrugged. "News travels fast around here, Mr. Santee. Is it supposed to be a secret?"

"No, apparently not. It's no big deal."

"Sounds big to me, especially on your 80th birthday."

Jack reasoned that even if two or three employees knew about his score, it wasn't likely that the birthday crowd would have a clue. He could decide later if he wanted to talk about his round or not.

A couple of other players walked into the Club Room, and Oscar excused himself to attend to them. Jack was ready to move to a corner table by himself anyway. It made sense to review the day's game while it was still fresh in his mind. He grabbed a pad of gin rummy score sheets from the bar, went to a secluded corner and flipped over the pad to start making notes.

On the other side of the clubhouse, the Hogan Room was a buzz of activity. Marie Santee had gone all out for Jack's 80th birthday, having chosen a golf theme for the night's proceedings. The room already featured several photos of Ben Hogan and other famous golfers on its walls documenting the times they had played at the Old Oak course. The florist had added golf flags to all of the table arrangements, while Marie had purchased green tablecloths and napkins with Scottish tartan patterns since all the club had to offer was white or black. For name placeholders, Marie had ordered place card golf balls that held the names for each guest, and in keeping with the theme, she wore a green knit cocktail suit with gold buttons.

A friend of theirs, Ted Anderson, arrived with an armload of blank signs. He was a retired political cartoonist, and Marie had asked him to make up some signs for the party. In short order, Ted knocked out several cartoonish caricatures showing Jack swinging a golf club and traversing the course. It took him about five minutes to make each sign, and Marie kept throwing him suggestions for additional scenes.

Everything was coming together quickly, Marie thought. She felt pleased with herself... she only hoped Jack's spirits would be up to the occasion.

Jack tapped the pad of paper with the butt of his pencil. He made a few notes about his round, then decided he wasn't in the mood to analyze anything further. He just wanted to enjoy the moment.

Jack sipped his drink and found himself circling around the question he had asked himself earlier: why had he wanted to break 80 on his 80th birthday? He felt that he had arrived at an answer at the Halfway House, but it now occurred to him that he might have also wanted to demonstrate to himself and others that the single-plane swing provided a better way to play enjoyable golf. That made sense. Also, his marketing background kept drawing him back to the phrase, "Breaking 80 at 80." *That might sell,* he thought. And if that goal worked well for an 80-year-old, why not for 50, 60 or 70-year-olds? It could also help out the surge of golfers who had recently taken up the game.

Jack realized he might be getting ahead of himself. It wasn't unusual for him to try to commercialize his hobbies by turning them into businesses. He habitually found himself with a surplus of imaginative ideas and not enough time or money to invest in them.

Oscar came up to Jack's table and interrupted his thoughts. "You'd better start getting ready for your party, Mr. Santee. It's 5:45 now, and I believe you're due at 6:15."

Jack glanced at the clock. Oscar was right. It never ceased to amaze him how well the club employees knew his schedule, right down to his locker room routines. Similarly, he was often thrown off by how causally the employees told members what to do.

"Thanks, Oscar." He ripped his notes off the pad, tucked them into his pocket and left to go take a shower.

Much of the day's stress had dissipated by the time Jack dried his hair and put on new clothes. After some internal debate, he decided to wear his green tie that had illustrations of gold bears on it - a bit eccentric, but the color matched his green sport coat nicely.

He checked his watch. 6:15, it read. *Whatever Marie is up to,* Jack thought, *she could probably use a few extra minutes.* He fussed with his thinning hair for a little while longer, then decided there was no use postponing the inevitable. He made one last adjustment to his tie, then packed up his locker and headed out into the hall.

As he made his way toward the Hogan Room, the day's events shuffled through Jack's mind. He realized how scattered his thinking had been regarding his quest. First, he had looked forward to breaking 80 and all the cocktail talk that would ensue. Then he'd considered keeping his score quiet whether he broke 80 or not. No doubt, he had wanted a cushion in case he fell short of his goal, but he also hadn't wanted to brag about his victory, if it had come to that. *Maybe,* he considered, *someone will just come up and ask me what I shot.* That was a ridiculous thought, Jack realized; his score would be the first question any of his old partners would ask.

The clubhouse seemed eerily quiet as Jack traversed the length of the building. Only after reaching the corridor that led to the Hogan Room did he start hearing the familiar sounds of a cocktail party. He hesitated at the doorway.

Well, you're only 80 once, Jack told himself. *Best try to enjoy it.*

And with that, Jack stepped into the room.

CHAPTER 20: THE HOGAN ROOM

*"Two roads diverged in a wood, and I — I took the one less
traveled by, and that has made all the difference."*
Robert Frost, American Poet

The first thing Jack saw, straight ahead, was a large sign
featuring a caricature of him in a golfer's stance. Below that
image was written, "HAPPY BIRTHDAY, MR. 79!".

Marie walked over from the side of the room and gave her
husband a big smile and an even bigger hug. "Happy birthday,
darling."

She took a step back from Jack, and both of them started
laughing when they realized they were wearing the same shade
of green. "We look like the Bobbsey twins," remarked Marie.

Jack pointed up at the number 79. "How did you know?"

She arched an eyebrow and looked at him as if he were a bit
slow. "You've been talking about it for five years, Jack."

"I have?"

"Yes, and maybe more. I wasn't sure if you were successful until I received word from the pro shop," she explained.

Jack remembered how fast the attendant had taken off when he turned his score in. *Oh.*

"Come on in." Marie slipped her arm around him. "Your friends are all here."

He left the entranceway and saw a long row of guests waiting to greet him. First in line were his old golf partners, Bob, Harry and John. They applauded and cried, "Congratulations!" simultaneously.

"I *thought* that was what you were up to today," Bob declared.

"*We all* did," Harry corrected. He turned back to Jack. "How could you keep a secret like that from your old friends?"

Jack gave some half-hearted protestations, and thankfully, he was saved by the appearance of two more familiar faces: the single-plane golf trainers Carl Johnson and Danny Murphy.

"Surprised to see us?" Carl asked.

"More than surprised," Jack admitted. "Especially you." Carl was notoriously averse to travel.

Jack suddenly remembered that he'd noticed someone he thought was Carl on the 17th fairway this morning. The other person in the cart must have been Danny. He questioned them about it.

"Yeah, we were trying to stay out of your sight," Danny explained.

"Thanks for coming." Jack shook their hands. "I can't believe you two are here."

Carl grinned. "It's always a boost to see one's students put their lessons to good use."

Jack felt a tap on his shoulder. He turned around, and standing there in front of him was his son, Jack Jr. They hugged warmly. "I thought I saw your BMW a few hours ago, but this morning you said you were calling from your office!"

"Forgive me for fibbing a little," said his son sheepishly. "I was actually on the road when I called, and you probably spotted me when I was headed for your house. I'd hoped you wouldn't see me."

Now Jack understood. "So, that's why your mom didn't want me to come home." He smiled proudly. "It means a lot for you to be here."

"Wouldn't miss it for the world."

Caught up in the excitement of seeing his son, Jack finally noticed another figure standing patiently behind him: the golf psychologist Dr. Michael Feinstein.

"Hello, Mr. 79," said Dr. Mike evenly. "Are you staying in the present?"

Jack shook his head a little as if to clear it. "I have no idea where I am."

"You deserve an out-of-body experience today," he said, giving the hint of a smile. "Happy birthday."

They shook hands. "Thanks for coming, Dr. Mike," said Jack. "You may very well be the guest who's traveled the longest distance."

Further conversation was interrupted when someone grabbed Jack's shoulders and spun him around. He found himself staring at Mr. High Tech Golf himself, the coach Ralph Williams.

"You did it, Jack!" Ralph beamed. "That's something pretty special... to break 80 on your 80th. You sure hyped it up a lot, and I knew you'd manage it sooner or later. Didn't expect it to happen today, but all the better!"

"Thanks," Jack said genuinely. "You were a big part of my success."

He continued to say hello to the other guests, all the while wondering if he had really let slip his secret about breaking 80 to so many people. *I guess I'm more talkative than I realized,* Jack admitted. He couldn't deny that at least ten friends knew about it even before they arrived at the party.

Cocktails were handed out for another forty-five minutes, and then Marie announced that it was time for everyone to sit at their assigned places. She had Jack take a seat at the center of the long table, and she sat to his right. Jack Jr. took the open chair to his left.

The guests had barely gotten settled when Bob pulled himself out of his seat and cleared his throat noisily. "I want to be the first to toast the Birthday Boy on his 80th," he said in his gravelly voice. "That way I can get it over with and get back to my drink." He sounded more serious than joking, though several people chuckled. "Jack – the only guy I know who has a golf psychologist and practices more than he plays. What a fanatic."

The audience laughed uncomfortably. With Bob, Jack could never tell whether the man was jesting or not. Thankfully, Bob ended with, "Here's to you, Jack. You're a good golfer and an even better friend."

Forks clinked against glasses in approval. Not to be outdone, John jumped up and drew the audience's attention. As usual, he pulled a poem of his own making out from his jacket and proceeded to read.

JACK, A MAN OF MANY ATTRIBUTES

WHICH TONIGHT WE GATHER TO SALUTE

BUT BREAKING EIGHTY AT HIS ADVANCED AGE

IS A FEAT WE RARELY HAVE SEEN STAGED

"Here's to Jack!" John concluded to more applause and cheers. Jack was relieved. Though of questionable grammar, it had been one of John's better and less vulgar poems.

Jack looked over and noticed a bit of irritation hiding behind Marie's careful expression. Undoubtedly, his wife thought that she, as the host, should have had the honor of making the opening toast. Perhaps she'd been planning to wait until after the first course had been served.

Jack Jr. reached behind his dad's chair and tapped his mother on the shoulder. "Better do it now," he told her, "before someone else pops up."

He knows his mother all too well, Jack thought to himself.

Marie stood and tapped her fork against her glass to gather everyone's attention. "I want to welcome and to thank all of you for coming tonight to Jack's party," she began. "Here's to Jack Santee... a wonderful husband and father..." She paused to let those first two accolades sink in. "and, I suppose I'm forced to admit, a pretty good golfer. Happy 80th birthday, dear."

The crowd erupted in a surge of applause and clinking of glasses. Jack thought he'd better respond. Knowing this group, someone else would try to make another toast and embarrass him further if he didn't speak up.

He got to his feet. "Welcome, everyone. First of all, I want to thank Marie for this wonderful party." He led the audience in applauding her, then resumed his speech. "I admit I knew about the party, but I didn't know about the golf theme. I didn't know there'd be these signs about breaking 80."

"That's my boy!" shouted Ralph from the end of the table.

Jack waited until the chuckles died down. "I thought I'd been keeping my goal a secret until I was reminded by many of you that I've been talking about this for some time." He paused to gather his words together. "When I was on the back nine today, I realized that if I didn't break 80, it wasn't going to be the end of my life. I have so much to be thankful for, and that includes all of you who took the time to be here tonight. Best wishes, and thank you for your support and friendship."

This time, Jack received a standing ovation. He hoped he had done the moment justice. He also hoped he'd said enough to forestall any further toasts, but the speeches kept coming as the dinner progressed. They congratulated him not only for his game but for his good health and his good fortune at having Marie as his wife.

For dessert, Marie had a large cake brought out with the shape of a golfer traced in icing on top next to the words, "Happy Birthday Mr. 79".

"How did you do that?" Jack asked her.

She smiled, quite pleased with herself. "I had the cake made here at the club. That way, the pastry chef could add the words at the last minute."

After a rousing chorus of "Happy Birthday", the distribution of cake and champaign and a final toast by Jack Jr., the guests gave their last regards and trickled away. Despite being a natural introvert, Jack felt immensely happy with the night's festivities. He'd weathered the crowd's attention just as he'd handled all the spectators who had shown up along the eighteen holes earlier today. Now he could fully appreciate having some time alone with his wife as they took down the decorations from the Hogan Room.

Marie had specifically mentioned *no presents,* but Jack's disobedient friends had left several behind on the table next to the few remaining slices of cake. The two of them gathered up the gifts and carried them out to their vehicles behind the clubhouse.

"So, what if I *hadn't* broken 80?" asked Jack as he opened her trunk.

Marie flashed him a cunning look. "That's easy. I would have had the pastry chef write, *Happy Birthday on your 80th*. And look in here." She showed him a large bag in her backseat that contained signs with more generic birthday messages. "We would have used those signs instead. Nothing else would have been different, Jack. The same decorations, the same food, and the same friends and family who care about you."

After the last presents had been stowed away, Jack leaned against her car and told her, "I can't thank you enough for tonight."

"You're welcome. It was my pleasure and done with love." She slipped in and gave him a kiss. "Are you still thinking about writing a book about today's adventure?"

"I am," he admitted. "But if I were to sum up the day, I think Moe Norman said it best: *The thrill is feeling the shot.*"

Jack knew he had begun to acquire a feeling for the single-plane swing. All his lessons, his dedication and his ambitions had paid off, and he resolved to keep his skills strong by hitting the course with more regularity.

It could only get better from here.

REFERENCES AND RECOMMENDED READING

Zen Golf by Dr. Joseph Parent
Doubleday, a division of Random House

The Single Plane Golf Swing by Todd Graves with Tim
O'Connor
Brown Books Publishing Group

The Feeling of Greatness (2nd Edition) by Tim O'Connor
Brown Books Publishing Group

The Legend of Moe Norman, The Man With the Perfect Swing
by Andrew Podnieks
Molydart Press

Finish to the Sky: The Golf Swing Moe Norman Taught to Me
by Greg Lavern

WHO WAS MOE NORMAN?

"I'm the best ball-striker the world has ever known. That's not me saying it. Ask all the pros who's the best." - Moe Norman

Murray Irwin "Moe" Norman (1929-2004) was a Canadian professional golfer from Kitchener, Ontario who was credited as the inventor of the single-plane swing.

Career Highlights:

- Canadian Amateur Championship winner (1955, 1956)
- 55 career Canadian Tour and other Canadian event victories
- Canadian PGA Championship winner (1966, 1974)
- Canadian PGA Seniors' Championship winner (1979-1985, 1987)
- 33 course records
- 17 holes-in-one
- Inducted into the Canadian Golf Hall of Fame in 1995

- Inducted into the Ontario Sports Hall of Fame in 1999
- Inducted into the Canada's Sports Hall of Fame in 2006

"I'll tell you about a guy who can hit it better than anybody. His name is Moe Norman up in Canada." - Tom Watson, American Professional Golfer

"Who is the best golfer I've ever seen? Moe Norman - he was incredible." - Vijay Singh, Fijian Professional Golfer

"When you talk about Moe Norman, you are talking about a legend. He's a legend with the professionals. I think the guy's a genius when it comes to playing the game of golf." - Lee Trevino, American Professional Golfer

ACKNOWLEDGMENTS

Many thanks to those who took the time to read the manuscript and offered encouragement and suggestions, including Steve Douglas, Frank McGinity, Joe Parent, Pat Pohlen, Robyn Puckett, Ken St. Clair, Bill Tomicki, and Kathy Whitworth.

A special note of gratitude to my editor Bryan Snyder who stayed with this project thru all the ups, downs, and delays. His golfing knowledge was rusty, but he always asked the right questions. Bryan continues to have a knack for deriving sense and order out of my words and phrases.

ABOUT THE AUTHOR

*Left to right: Wes St. Clair, Tournament Chairman and Founder of The
Southgate Open, Ralph Davis, Tournament Director, Carol Mann LPGA
Member 38 wins (1941-2018), Kathy Whitworth LPGA Member 88
wins (1939-), Mickey Wright LPGA Member 82 wins (1935-2020) - all
inductees of the World Golf Hall of Fame, Cynthia Sullivan, President of
the LPGA in 1970 (1937-2020)*

Wes St. Clair has been involved with the sport of golf for many
decades and has been a member of various golf clubs throughout
the country. In recent years, he has been more of a student of
golf than a player, always intrigued with various swings and the

effectiveness of those swings. From 1969 to 1975, Wes was the founder and chairman of the Southgate Open - a Ladies Professional Golf Tournament (LPGA) held in the Kansas City region. He is the author of *A Story About a Ranch* and currently resides in the Salt Lake City area.